Finding Home

Annie Seaton

Love Across Time series
1. Come Back to Me
2. Follow Me
3. Finding Home
4. The Threads that Bind (2021)

This book is a work of fiction. Names, characters, places, magazines and incidents are the product of the author's imagination or are used fictitiously. Any resemblance to actual events, locales, or persons, living or dead, is coincidental.

Copyright © November 2020 by Annie Seaton.

DEDICATION

This book is dedicated to the historical authors whose works I have read and loved over many years.

Chapter 1

Fat bumble bees buzzed around the garden as Alice McLaren kicked her boot against the bottom of the high brick wall. The last of the summer roses tumbled down the red bricks, and the sharp smell of violets sweetened the late afternoon air.

But it didn't sweeten her mood. It wasn't fair; Mother would never let her go into the fields and explore behind their house.

Never, ever.

Alice knew there were wonderful things to be seen on the other side of that wall, but Mother said she was not to go there, *ever*, and Daddy nodded wisely, deferring to Mother as he *always* did.

That wall was a barrier between the back garden of Violet Cottage and the magical world beyond. Alice stood there and stared at the solid brick. No matter how high she tried to climb on the chairs on the back porch when Mother wasn't looking, she still couldn't see over the top of the wall. She was not allowed to go into her parents' bedroom. Alice was sure she would be able to see over the wall from there, because that was their private space, Mother said.

Frustration tugged at Alice and she stamped her foot. She could hear the cows mooing and the birds singing on the other side, and if she listened extra carefully, she was sure she could hear little voices. But she couldn't *see.*

Mother even went with her along the road as she walked to the village school in Pilton each morning; it would have been much quicker to cut across the fields and through the forest, but no, she wasn't allowed to.

Maybe Mother feared the creatures in there. Perhaps that was why there was no gate in the wall. Alice was sure there had been a gate there once because there were different coloured bricks in a rectangle in the middle. She had learned what a rectangle was at school, and someone had made one in the wall with new bricks.

'I'm not scared,' she muttered crossly. 'I could go into the fields.'

Before Granny McLaren had died last year, every night for as long as Alice could remember, her father's mother had told her many stories about the enchanted forest behind the cottage where the McLaren family had lived for a long, long time.

Right back to the fifteenth century, Granny would say, with a wide smile, her deep wrinkles fascinating Alice.

Wizards and goblins, witches and elves, lived in the fields, and one of Granny's stories even had a leprechaun coming over from Ireland to see the blue light that warmed the magical creatures. Those magical creatures who made their home in the forest on the other side of this wall.

Granny would know, because she had lived in this cottage since she had been a young woman, and married Grandfather. Alice didn't remember him; he had gone to sleep when she was a baby, but there was a picture of him on the mantelpiece.

'Mummy, can you tell me a story please?' Alice asked one night not long after they had buried Granny in the village cemetery in Glastonbury. The fire was crackling in the hearth in the living room and seeing Granny's empty chair beside the fire made Alice sad. 'I miss Granny. Why did she have to go to sleep?'

'Because she was old and ready to have her eternal rest,' Mother said with her lips pursed as she sewed the hem of Alice's school dress.

'What's eternal?' Alice screwed her face up. The vicar had said that word too when Granny was sleeping in that wooden box at the front of the church.

Before they put her in the ground.

That had made Alice shiver. She wasn't going to ever have that long sleep and be put in the ground.

Mother had allowed her to go to the church when they said goodbye to Granny. Alice had worn her new black wool dress, with the scratchy long underwear beneath it that Granny had knitted, and her new stockings were held up by an uncomfortable thing that was stuck on the bottom of her underwear. When she had asked for the yellow ribbon to tie back her hair, Mother had made a tsking noise, and brushed her hair so hard, it brought tears to Alice's eyes.

'No colour today, Alice. We must show respect.'

Life in their cottage had changed since Granny had gone to sleep, and Alice hated the way things were now.

'A story about the forest, please, Mother,' she asked again.

'No, Alice.' Mother turned to Daddy. 'Your mother filled that child's head with nonsense.'

'It wasn't nonsense.' Alice stamped her foot and her mother turned to her mending. Daddy was reading the newspaper and looked at her over his round spectacles. As much as she loved him, and he brought a halfpenny of sweets and the *School Friends* comic home for her every Friday afternoon, Alice knew Daddy would never stand up to Mother.

'Granny told me about the creatures that live there,' Alice persisted. 'I want to hear some more about them.'

'There are no creatures, and they were only stories that Granny told you. She made them up.' Mother put her mending down. 'You are almost eight-years-old,

Alice, and that is old enough not to need silly stories any longer.' She looked up at the old grandfather clock that had stood in the corner of the cottage for hundreds and hundreds of years, Granny had told her.

'It fills your head with rubbish,' Mother said. 'No wonder you have nightmares. No more stories. It's time you were in bed.'

If only she could get into the forest, she would know that Granny's stories were true. She would prove it to Mother and maybe that would make her smile.

No yellow ribbon. No colour. They were the right words. All the colour had gone since Granny had gone, and Alice was determined to bring it back and make Mother smile again.

Alice kicked at the fence again and jumped aside when a brick fell past her head. It tumbled to the ground and landed in three pieces on the grass beside her boot. Boots that she would have to polish, now that she had scuffed them.

She looked down at the broken fragments of brick and then leaned her head back trying to see where it had come from. Goose bumps rose on her neck as excitement filled her. There was a gap in the wall about halfway up.

Alice looked around for something to stand on; it was too far to pull the heavy chair down from the porch. Her gaze settled on the wooden barrow that old

Mr Jenkins next door used when he did the gardening each Monday afternoon. If she emptied it out, and tipped it over, she could stand on it, and she *might* be able to reach the new hole in the wall.

Alice ran over to the barrow and lifted the garden trimmings out with her bare hands, throwing them onto the newly mown grass. A sharp pain pierced the end of her thumb and she cried out. For a moment, she thought a bee had stung her. She looked down and gasped as a dark red drop of blood welled from her thumb. A rose thorn had pierced the skin, and she widened her eyes with dismay as another drop of blood ran down her palm.

Not deterred by the blood, Alice wiped her hand on the edge of her skirt and then pulled her handkerchief out and wound it around her thumb. Nothing, not even a throbbing thumb was going to stop her climbing the wall and looking into the magic forest.

But she had to hurry, the sun had almost set, and Mother would soon be calling her in for her supper. She looked to the west and the spires of Glastonbury church glinted in the slanting sunlight.

With renewed determination, Alice turned back to the barrow, but this time she was more careful as she lifted the last of the grass clippings and rose clippings onto the grass.

Her mouth turned down as she looked at the mess she had deposited on the lawn, and she knew she would have to put it all back when she had finished.

With a worried glance back at the cottage Alice let out a sigh; smoke was curling lazily from the chimney which meant that Mother had lit the stove to cook supper. She would have to hurry. Quickly she turned the barrow around and wheeled it down to the wall. Anticipation surged through her as she slowly turned it over and clambered up onto it. She pressed her palms flat against the bricks; the gap was just above her eyes. If she stood on her tiptoes, she should be able to reach the opening. The bricks were warm against her hands as she supported herself and pushed up onto her toes. Alice's hands were shaking, and she stretched as high as she could, trying to keep her balance on the sloping back of the wooden barrow. Closing her left eye, she leaned forward and pressed her right eye to the gap.

A disappointed gasp broke from her lips as a wide vista of green fields filled her narrow vision. Four black and white cows ambled slowly across the field towards the one tree in the middle of the field. There was no forest, and there were no magical creatures to be seen.

One lone beech tree soared into the early evening sky, the leaves dappled with late golden sunlight. Maybe the magical creatures lived in the huge tree,

Alice wondered, determined not to give up on what she believed in. Granny wouldn't have told her lies; she was determined to believe in the magic.

Alice pressed her face harder against the wall and blinked as the sun disappeared below St Michael's Tower on Glastonbury Tor and a bright flash of blue light blinded her for a moment. She blinked again.

The magic light! She knew Granny's stories had been true.

Alice screwed up her face and closed her eyes as she thought hard. The farmer must have cut down all the trees after Granny died, and only left one tree for the cows to sleep under.

Opening her eyes Alice looked to the left where the light was coming from. Three tall stones tinted with a bluish light stood in a row to the left of the tree.

'Alice, where are you? Your supper is ready.' Her mother's voice drifted down from the cottage, but she didn't sound cross.

Yet.

Alice pulled back from the wall, and slid down the barrow, before running back to the cottage as fast as her short legs would take her.

'I'm coming, Mother,' she called. 'I'll wash my hands out here.' She slipped into the washhouse that was off the back porch. Taking her shoes off, she left them beside Daddy's black gumboots, ready to polish in the morning.

She would have to come out in the dark after her parents were asleep and put the clippings back into the barrow, so they didn't know what she had been doing. Alice was determined to go into that field now that she had seen Granny's stories were true.

Excitement tingled down to her toes as she washed her bloodstained handkerchief and left it on the stone washtub to dry. Even her sore thumb was forgotten as Alice remembered that magical light.

'Thank you, Granny,' she whispered as she headed in for her supper.

Chapter 2

'Alice Mary McLaren!'

Alice was sitting on her bed looking at the comic book that her father had brought home from town last night. She bit her lip and sat completely still; the tone of her mother's voice informed her that she had done something wrong.

Again.

Scrunching up her eyes, she tried to remember what she could have forgotten. She had brushed her teeth last night and had done her chores: the kindling was by the stove ready for this morning, and she had put milk in the saucer for the cat.

Her breath caught as she thought about her boots; how she had scuffed them yesterday afternoon when she had kicked the brick wall and climbed on the barrow.

And seen the magic light.

Oh dear. And left a mess in the back garden.

After she had had her supper last night, Alice had washed her face, climbed into her bed and gone straight to sleep; all thoughts of going out and putting the clippings back in the barrow had fled. Her dreams had been full of elves and leprechauns, and now that she had seen the huge beech tree where they lived, she was even more determined to go into the fields and explore.

Mother had obviously been into the back garden and seen the mess of garden clippings and Alice knew she was in trouble. She slipped quietly off the bed and padded to the door in her stockinged feet. She could hear her parents talking in the garden beneath her window.

'Why would she do that?' Mother asked. 'No good reason, apart from making more work for Mr Jenkins. That child needs punishing.'

Alice's bottom lip quivered. How could she have forgotten about the barrow last night? Her father's voice was a low murmur, but she couldn't hear what he was saying. All she hoped was that they didn't notice the gap in the wall.

Had she moved the barrow away?

Drat. She couldn't remember.

Oh, she was in such big trouble.

Hurrying back to her bed, she picked up the comic book, and then quietly opened her bedroom door. She walked down the steps on her tiptoes and stepped to the right when she reached the third bottom step that always creaked.

She paused in the hall and listened, reassuring herself that her parents were still in the garden.

'She's emptied that barrow and used it to try to climb the wall.' Mother's voice came through the window. They were still in the back garden.

'Don't be silly, Kathryn. She knows she can't reach the top.'

'She takes after you, Henry. And your mother. Always daydreaming. It is not healthy for a young girl to be like that.'

'She is a child. And that is what children do. Dream and imagine. You are too hard on her.'

'And while ever we live in this place I will continue to be so.'

Alice scurried through the hall, grabbed an apple from the wooden fruit bowl on the kitchen table and quietly slid open the latch on the low door next to the wood stove.

The cellar off the kitchen was Alice's place for hiding when Mother was in one of her moods. Opening the door, she slipped in and closed it behind her. There was a chink of light coming beneath it from the kitchen, so there would be just enough light for her to finish reading her comic.

Father kept his wine in here, but Mother was a teetotaller, so the cellar door was rarely opened, except by Alice.

'Alice! Come down here now.' Mother's footsteps echoed on the wooden floor as she came inside and walked past the cellar.

The third step from the bottom creaked as she went upstairs. Alice held her breath, and when Mother came back down a few minutes later her footsteps were quicker and heavier.

'Henry, she's not there. I've looked everywhere. Under her bed, and in the bathroom, and in our bedroom.'

'Calm down.' Daddy's voice was firm but held a note of worry. 'She won't be far away.'

'I'll look down here, you go out into the garden and look along the road,' Mother said.

For a moment, Alice considered coming out of her hidey-hole, the distress in Mother's voice made her feel bad for hiding.

The back door opened, and Daddy's voice was quiet as it always was. 'Keep calm, Kathryn. She won't be far away. I'll check the garden. You put the kettle on. I can't be late for work today.'

Alice's eyes widened as Mother yelled. She never yelled at Daddy.

'Forget about work, and cups of tea. What if she's gone into the fields?' Her voice rose in pitch as she spoke faster. 'What if she's found the gate on the ley line? What if she's gone too? I told you it was too dangerous to stay in this cottage, and then your mother filled her head with all that nonsense. Am I the only one who sees the danger of living near a time gate with a young child? And a child with a head for daydreaming? A child who is desperate to go into those bloody fields.'

A chair scraped on the flagstones and then to Alice's deeper shame—she had never heard Mother swear before—loud sobs came through the closed cellar door.

Alice took a deep breath and stood up, brushing the dust off her pyjamas. Opening the door quietly, she peered around. Mother was sitting at the table with her head in her hands. Daddy stood there with his hand on her shoulder.

Alice climbed out of the cellar and crept over and reached up and tugged at her mother's hand. 'It's all right, Mummy. I'm here. I'm not missing.'

Her mother reached for her and held her tight. 'Oh, thank God.'

'Mummy? What's a time gate?' Alice asked.

Chapter 3

Not long after the afternoon the brick had fallen out of the wall in the back garden at Violet Cottage, the McLaren family moved to a flat in Lower Sydenham, London. Alice was eight-years-old. The memories of the cottage and the fields and the magical creatures faded, but Alice always promised herself she would return there one day.

They had never once been back to the cottage to visit, and as she grew older, Alice could not understand why they stayed in London when they owned a pretty cottage with a garden in the country. Especially when Alice was eighteen and the war began in 1939, and it became unsafe to venture out in the streets, or indeed, stay inside.

Alice and Kathryn spent many nights of the ninety-day bombing blitz of late 1940 in the Anderson shelter at the bottom of the garden.

'It reminds me of the cellar in the cottage in Somerset,' Alice said one night as the bombs fell around them. Keeping Mother talking helped to keep her calm. 'Perhaps we should go back there until the war is over,' Alice said.

Mother shook her head and looked at Alice strangely. 'No, we are safer here.'

'We could go down there and take some London children in,' Alice had suggested again when the danger in the city intensified and children began to be evacuated to the country. 'You should see them, Mummy. It makes me so sad.' Alice had left her position as a shorthand-typist and joined the Women's Volunteer Service. She helped marshal the children in preparation for evacuation to the country. 'They are so frightened and upset. I had to comfort a woman yesterday at Paddington station. Three of her children were being sent down to a farm in Devon.'

'The times are very hard, but it would be safer for them there,' her mother said.

'The poor woman cried in my arms for half an hour after the train had departed. If we went down to Somerset, we would have room in the cottage to take in three or four little ones, and we would be much safer out of London.'

'No, Alice. We will stay here with your father. He needs us. And besides Somerset has been bombed too. Westlands Airfield has been a target of the *Luftwaffe, and* who knows how many Germans are wandering around the countryside. No, we are safer here and we will stay with your father.'

Because of his asthma, Henry had not been accepted into the army, and was involved in special work for the government.

His work was top secret, and even Mother didn't know what he did or where he spent his days. It was not unusual for Henry to stay away from their flat for three or four days at a time as bombs dropped on the city day after day.

Alice knew there was no point arguing. She loved her father, but they rarely saw him.

Tragedy struck on Christmas Eve in 1940 after weeks and weeks of relentless bombing. The noise of the German planes became commonplace as they flew over London incessantly, skimming roof tops, and the air was permanently filled with the smell of explosives. The whistle of the falling bombs left Kathryn shaking and nauseated, but no matter how hard Alice tried, she could not convince her mother to leave the city.

Very few buses were running, so Henry walked to the office where he worked, and on Christmas Eve, 1940, after a particularly intense three days of bombing, there came a loud knock at the door of their flat.

'I'm very sorry, Mrs McLaren, I regret to inform you . . .'

The words circled around in Alice's head as she held her mother. Daddy had been killed in a bombing raid three nights before. While they had waited for him to come home, he had already been dead.

One morning a week later, they were still in shock and Alice slipped out quickly to get some milk from the shop at the end of the street. She froze as the sirens sounded and the bombs whistled and there was an almighty explosion close by. Running down the road, milk forgotten, she was confronted by smoking rubble where their flat had once been. She knew that her mother would not have had a chance to get to the shelter, but still she dropped to her knees and dug with her bare hands until her fingers bled.

At nineteen, Alice McLaren was left alone, both her parents victims of the Blitz.

##

'I think that's a very sensible idea, love.' Maureen Barnstaple, the centre organiser for evacuation stood beside Alice in the rest centre where they provided food and drink to the wardens and firefighters fighting the fires caused by the bombing. 'Where is your family's cottage?'

'It's halfway between Pilton and Glastonbury in Somerset. I haven't been there since I was a child, but I know Violet Cottage is empty, and has been looked after by the owners of the cottage next door. Or at least I think it has. There is a big back garden so as well as taking children in, I could grow vegetables.' Her voice broke. 'There is no reason for me to stay in London now.'

'I think it's a very wise move. We'll miss you here, you've been a wonderful worker. Do you have family down there too?'

Alice shook her head and tried not to sound as though she was seeking sympathy. 'There is no one. Both sets of my grandparents passed when I was a child, and my parents had no siblings. My father had one uncle, and I believe he had children, but I have never met them.'

'I am so sorry to hear that, love. But as you have nowhere to live now, it does make sense to move to your family's cottage.' Maureen's smile was kind. 'I know where it is. My husband's family hails from Somerset. Why don't you travel down and see what condition the cottage is in, and then let us know if you can take any children. It would be silly to send them down with you, sight unseen.'

'I will. I'll leave tomorrow and I'll be in touch as soon as I can.' Alice reached out and put her hand on Maureen's arm. 'Thank you for letting me stay with you. I don't know what I would have done without your support. I still can't believe—' Her voice broke and she put her hands up to her face.

Maureen put her arms around Alice and held her close to her soft matronly bosom. 'Oh, get away with you, love. It's the least Jim and I could do. We've enjoyed your company over these past three months.'

Alice nodded and pulled back and wiped her eyes, embarrassed to be crying in the evacuation centre where everyone could see her.

Losing both her parents within a week, as well as her home, had left her in a state of shock.

She was alone in the world now. A very dangerous and horrid world.

Chapter 4

Alice stared at her reflection in the grimy window of the train, barely aware of the fields flashing past as the train headed towards Somerset. The weather was miserable; grey heavy skies threatened snow that she was hoping would hold off until she reached the cottage.

Alice was concerned about going back to the cottage, worried that she was making the wrong decision. Not having been back once in the past eleven years made her wonder how well it had been looked after. The move to London had been good for them. The one thing that stayed with her as the train approached Castle Cary station was how much happier her mother had been after they moved to London.

Once they were settled in their flat in Lower Sydenham, Mother had become a different person, and their lives had changed. It hadn't taken Alice long to get used to the traffic and crowds in London, and she'd loved exploring the city.

She'd had a wonderful childhood, and the memories of those years getting to know the soft, kind person that her mother became would stay with her forever.

The strain that had been etched on Kathryn's face had disappeared when they had moved to the city, and their flat had been filled with laughter.

Daddy would sit there at night trying to read the *Times* and listen to the BBC, but more often than not he would give up and join in whatever game they were playing.

Mother had taken Alice to see much of London every school holiday. Their knowledge of this wonderful city grew as they took in a different sight every Saturday in school term: museums, art galleries, tiny bookstores hidden in alleyways—Mother knew where to find all of the interesting out of the way attractions.

'I am going to travel the world when I grow up,' she had informed her mother on her twelfth birthday. 'I do love seeing new things.'

Mummy had smiled her gentle smile. 'I hope you do, darling. There are many things to see.'

As war had threatened her, parents had looked increasingly worried and had listened to BBC radio every day, and Alice's concerns grew too.

And inevitably war had come, and their lives—her life—had changed irrevocably.

At quarter past eleven, on the morning of Sunday 3 September 1939, Broadcasting House in London faded-out the sound of *Bow Bells* and switched to number ten Downing Street. Prime Minister Neville Chamberlain spoke to the nation and he announced that, as Hitler had failed to respond to British demands to leave Poland, 'This country is at war with Germany.'

Alice swallowed as an unbearable pang of grief lodged behind her breastbone. She put her hand there and rubbed slowly trying to ease the pain, but it stayed.

Oh, she missed Mother's laughter so much, and Daddy's gentle smile as he had looked over his spectacles at his wife. Her parents had loved each other so much, and that was the one thing that helped console Alice. One day she hoped to find a love as deep as the one that her parents had shared. At least they hadn't had to grieve the loss of each other.

The loss of her parents was hard to comprehend, and she would miss them both dreadfully; she and Mother had been more like friends than mother and daughter over the past few years.

Alice closed her eyes for a while, but the rattle of the train kept her awake. She leaned down and took her notebook from the bag on the floor by her feet. When she was thirteen, she had begun to chronicle her days, and it cheered her to go back and read about the days before the war when she and Mother had explored the city.

Alice had always loved the pomp and ceremony of the changing of the guard, which happened daily at Buckingham Palace when the king was in residence. They would get the train to Green Park station at least once every week, always exclaim over the sheep in Green Park, and then would stand at the gates of the palace while Alice dreamed of meeting a prince one day. The problem was there were no princes, only the two young princesses.

She read her entry for the king's birthday two years ago when they had attended the Trooping of the Colour.

Mother nudged me and pointed to the east of the gate and I drew a breath as the carriage holding the little princesses accompanied by Queen Mary came into view. We had heard that Queen Elizabeth had a cold, so mother wasn't interested in staying longer than we had to, but I loved every moment of it. The crowd was huge and lots of people have periscopes, but Mother and I always knew to head for the gate from where we had an uninterrupted view. King George VI was on horseback and he led the Scots Guards down the Mall from Buckingham Palace and then saluted at the Horse Guards as the ceremony continued.

Mother took my hand. 'Come on, Alice, we'll go and have tea before the crowds leave.'

A military band marched across the parade ground and I shook my head.

'Just a few more minutes, Mummy. Look, Queen Mary and the princesses are watching from a window.'

I pointed to the window on the second floor and I would swear that they looked straight at me. Mother laughed and dragged me away.

'Come on, we're going to have a cream cake each with our cup of tea.'

Alice sighed, rested the notebook on her lap and rummaged in her bag for the lead pencil that she always carried with her.

She wrote the date in looping letters:

April 5th, 1941.

Today is the first day of my new life. I will be strong and independent. I will make a life for myself in the country. I will live a life that would have made my parents proud.

She lifted her pencil and stared through the window. The sky had darkened, and she fought the sadness that her thoughts and words had let creep in. She picked up the pen.

There will be no princes for me, and when the war is over and it is safe again, I will travel. I will see Europe and I may even live in Italy for a while.

Mummy had dreamed of that, and I will follow her dream for her.

She blinked back the tear that threatened to spill over. Alice knew that her inheritance would allow her to travel, and she would always have Violet Cottage as her home.

If this blasted war ever ended.

Chapter 5

Light snow was falling as Alice waited at the railway station at Castle Cary. She had learned that the only taxi had taken one passenger on a short trip to the next village and it would return for her.

'Don't worry, miss. I told him to come back and he will,' the stationmaster assured her. 'Go into the waiting room. It will be warmer in there than out on the road. We've had such good weather this past week, it's hard to believe we're having snow again. Hopefully this is the last of it.'

Alice sat down with her case next to her stockinged legs and rubbed her gloved hands together as the wind whistled through the open doorway on each side of the waiting room. A gas fire in the corner glowed brightly but did not generate much heat. Blackout curtains covered the square windows, and one lone bulb hung from the ceiling and bathed the small room in dim light. Alice couldn't see the point of the curtains as there were no doors to the waiting room.

Her stomach rumbled as the stationmaster stood in the doorway, and her cheeks heated. She had barely eaten over the last few days. Maureen Barnstaple had packed a parcel of supplies for her to bring down with her, but she hadn't even looked at them. They were safely in her case, along with the underwear, stockings and two dresses that had been given to her. Everything Alice owned had been lost when the flat was bombed. Luckily, she had taken her bag with her to the shop and had not lost her precious notebook.

'I've just boiled the kettle on the hob in my office. I'll bring you a cup of tea, lass. There'll be time,' the stationmaster said.

'Thank you, you're very kind.'

'We have to look out for each other in this war, don't we?' His large moustache bobbed as he nodded. 'You're off to Pilton, you said? Family there?'

'It is our family cottage, but there is no one waiting for me.'

A few minutes after he'd left her, he came back carrying a large mug of tea in one hand and a piece of buttered bread in the other. Under one arm, there was a brown paper package, and once Alice had taken the mug and the bread from him, he put it on the floor next to her suitcase.

'Just a few things to see you through until you settle in.'

'Thank you so much,' she said wrapping her gloved hands around the hot mug. Voices came in from the platform, and he gave her a quick smile and went out.

Alice stared down at the parcel. Food was the last thing she had considered when she had packed to come down to the cottage, until Maureen had gently reminded her that there would be nothing in the cottage. She had a vague memory of a village shop that Mother had taken her to when she was a little girl, and she hoped it was still there, and that she would be able to remember where it was. She wasn't even sure she would remember which way the village was.

Alice had just finished the hot tea, and put the mug on the seat beside her, when the stationmaster returned. 'Your taxi is here, love. I told him where you need to go. Joe is an honest man; he will charge you a reasonable fare.'

The taxi was waiting outside the station, and Joe, the driver, got out and insisted on taking her case and the food parcel. Alice clutched her small bag to her chest as she slipped into the back seat of the taxicab. The notebook was the last link to her parents and she never let it out of her sight.

'Violet Cottage at Pilton, love?' he asked as he clambered into the driver's seat.

'Yes, thank you.'

Despite her best intentions, and her curiosity to see if the route was familiar, Alice drifted off to sleep in the warmth of the taxi. The roads were dark, and she wouldn't have seen anything anyway.

It wasn't long before the taxi pulled up and she stirred. The snow was caught in the dim lights of the taxi; the ground was already white as the snow began to fall in earnest.

'We're here. Violet Cottage. Looks like there's nobody home.'

'No,' she said, taking her case from him. 'No, there's not.' She took a pound note from her purse and handed it to him.

'Thanks, love. Will you be all right here by yourself?' He handed her the change.

'I will be.'

She stood there as the taxi drove off and then turned to the cottage where she had been born and spent the first eight years of her life.

The outline of the two-storey cottage was visible in the soft moonlight that appeared occasionally through the scudding clouds.

Alice sighed. How much longer would this war last? It had been over a year since she had seen a house or a street lit with anything stronger than a subdued light.

Her shoulders slumped as weariness and despair filled her. A cold gust of wind blew in from the north as Alice picked up her case and opened the gate of the cottage. Her mood improved as the hinges creaked, and a memory came back.

'Henry, I swear if you don't stop that gate creaking, I'll oil it myself.'

Daddy had smiled. 'And then you won't hear anyone coming to the door until they knock, my darling.'

Her mother had rolled her eyes. 'And what would that matter, you silly man?'

'It gives you time to put the kettle on.'

Alice reached the door and her heart was lighter. Being here would let her leave the grief of London behind, and hopefully there would be many more happy memories recalled by simply being in the cottage.

She put her case down and looked around. If there was a key to this door in London, it had been lost in the devastation of their flat.

Once Mother's body had been retrieved from the rubble by the firemen, Alice had not been back to their street. An Air Raid Precaution warden had taken her to the evacuation centre.

She hadn't been able to face going back to the street where they had lived. Her fingers were still healing from her frantic digging. The smell of burning flesh and the sight of mutilated bodies would not leave her. There was no hysteria or screaming that day; the look of utter helplessness on the faces of those who had survived in Kingsthorpe Road had reflected her devastation.

With a deep sigh, Alice went to the side of the small porch hoping that the spare key was still where it had always been when they lived here. It had been her job as a child to get the key from beneath the cobblestone in the corner of the porch when Mummy had walked her home from the village school.

The cobblestone was hard to move, and her injured fingers throbbed as she loosened it and reached underneath. A rare smile lifted her lips as her hand encountered the cold metal of the front door key. As far as she knew, her parents had not been back to the cottage and they paid Mr Jenkins next door to keep an eye on it and keep the garden tidy.

She wondered why they had never visited before the war. It wasn't that far from London, and she and Mother had taken many train trips to the country when Daddy was at work through the week.

One of her favourite places had been the Lakes District and when the war was over, she would go back and explore all the lakes. Alice was very fortunate that her parents had left her financially comfortable. The family solicitor had sought her out as soon as he had read of the deaths of her parents in the *Times.*

Alice slid the key into the lock; her eyes were becoming more accustomed to the dark the longer she was there. She jumped as something scurried on the path behind her, and she quickly turned the key.

Chapter 6

A watery ray of sunlight dancing on the wall of the living room was the first thing that Alice saw when she opened her eyes the following morning. The cottage was cold, and her legs ached where they were tucked beneath the cushions of the sofa. She had not been game to explore the cottage in the dark last night and had felt her way to where she remembered the sofa had been. Today she would look for candles and see if there was any oil in the lamps she remembered being in the two bedrooms. She would have to find something to cover the windows too and search out and air some bed linen and blankets.

Last night she had kicked her shoes off, and wrapping her wool coat around her, had pulled some of the sofa cushions over and curled into a tight ball as tiredness consumed her. The dusty smell had made her sneeze a few times, but she hadn't taken long to fall asleep.

A familiar patterned wallpaper and a large grandfather clock in the corner met her gaze as Alice sat up and looked around. The room was the same as she remembered it, although everything seemed much smaller. She stood and stretched and began her exploration of Violet Cottage.

As she stood at the base of the stairs the cold of the flagstones was a shock to her stockinged feet. Holding the polished banister, she took a deep breath and walked up the staircase, smiling as the third step creaked. At the top of the stairs was a narrow hall and three doors leading to two bedrooms and a tiny bathroom. She opened the door to the bathroom in search of a lavatory, and then smiled again. Her memories of the cottage hadn't included the outdoor lavatory behind the washhouse. It was something she had taken for granted as a child and had quickly forgotten as they had become used to the luxuries of electric power, an inside lavatory, and plumbing to the kitchen and bathroom when they had moved to the city. And she had forgotten the pump at the well in the back garden where her father had pumped water for their use each day.

No wonder Mother had been keen to move to London. Their life there had had luxuries that Alice knew she had quickly taken for granted.

Alice walked back down the stairs and slipped her shoes on and went in search of the remembered lavatory; she would look in the bedrooms later once she had decided what she needed from the village.

If she could indeed find the village.

So far, being in the cottage had not made her feel too sad, but she wasn't ready to step into the room that had been her parents' bedroom.

Mr Jenkins or someone else must have been taking care of the cottage; the back garden was tidy, and there was a zinc pan full of fresh, clean water outside the washhouse.

When she came out of the lavatory, Alice washed her face and hands in the icy water and stood looking out across the garden. The snow had stopped overnight, and now there was just a wet sludge beneath her feet as she made her way to the birdbath in the centre of the grass. Someone must have been here this morning as two red-breasted robins pecked at crumbs that had been left on the circular stone bath.

The birds looked at her curiously, unbothered by her presence as she stood and watched them.

'Hello there.'

Alice turned as a call came from across the low brick wall between the two cottages. She walked across the wet grass and the man on the other side approached his side of the wall. As he came closer, she recognised him. Even though it had been eleven years, Mr Jenkins looked the same, apart from the deeper lines etched in his face.

'Good morning,' she said when she reached the fence. Mr Jenkins was holding a pair of gardening shears and on the other side of his garden was a pile of dead tree boughs.

'Are you looking for someone, miss? There's no one lives in Violet Cottage anymore.'

'I know.'

As he looked at her his eyes narrowed, and a smile slowly spread across his face.

'Alice? Little Alice McLaren all grown up?'

'Yes, Mr Jenkins. It's me.'

'Oh lass, I can see that now. You have such a look of your mother.'

Alice drew a breath and her lip trembled. 'Thank you, it's very good to hear that.'

'What are you doing down in Somerset? Last correspondence I had from your father, he said you were working as a shorthand-typist.'

She nodded. 'I was before the war.'

'It's been a while since I heard from him. Ah, the bloody war,' he said. 'I'm sorry I shouldn't swear, but we've not been immune to it down here. We've been a lot more careful since Coventry was bombed. Did your parents come down with you? I've been looking after the place as best I can.'

Alice nodded slowly. 'I can see that.' Taking a deep breath, she managed to get the words out. 'I came down alone in the train last night. I'm sorry to have to tell you that my parents were killed in separate incidents at Christmas. Daddy was at work, and a week later my mother was in our flat when our street was bombed. That's why I'm here; there is nothing to keep me in London. I'm going to live down here now.'

Mr Jenkins shook his head slowly. 'I am so very sorry to hear that, lass. Come around and have a cup of tea with me. I'll put the kettle on. Watch out for my small dog when you come through the gate. Cyril doesn't bite but he will bark at you and pretend to be vicious.'

'Cyril?' she asked wiping away the tears that had welled as she had told him of her parents' death.

Mr Jenkins chuckled, but Alice had seen him wipe away a tear too. 'He already had a name when I got him. He was my sister's dog.'

'Was?' she asked.

'My sister was killed in September. In an air raid on the south coast. She was eighty, and no one else wanted Cyril, so I took him. He's been good company for me. Anyway lass, come on around, and I'll catch you up on our local news.'

Alice went back in through the cottage and brushed her hair before opening her case and taking out the food parcel Maureen had packed. She knew that food was rationed, and she was pleased to find a small wedge of fruit cake wrapped in brown paper. Taking it with her, she opened the front door, and stepped onto the porch.

Alice hesitated, wondering if she should lock the door behind her, but as she looked along the road, she could see there was no one in sight, so she pulled it closed without locking it.

True to Mr Jenkins' word, a small dog yapped at her as she opened the front gate of his cottage. She crouched down, careful to keep the cake out of his reach as she scratched beneath his chin with her free hand. 'Hello, Cyril, you're a fine-looking chap.' The dog stopped barking and wagged his little tail. Alice stood and waited on the front porch.

'Come on in, Alice. I'm out back.'

The kettle was whistling as she made her way through the living room. Both cottages were identical, and she found her way to the kitchen easily. Mr Jenkins was pouring boiling water into a large teapot. Everything looked familiar as she looked around. A Welsh dresser filled with crockery was against the wall next to the back door, half covering the window. She walked over and picked up a blue china bell.

'I used to come over here and visit when we lived next door, didn't I? I remember playing with this bell,' she said. 'And Mrs Jenkins would give me lemonade and fairy cakes. I'd forgotten so much about living at Violet Cottage. I was so sorry when we left to go to London. Is Mrs Jenkins . . .'

'Mrs Jenkins passed seven years ago,' he said as he gestured to a chair.

'I'm very sorry to hear that,' she said.

'Sit down, lass. It's not a bad thing. She was ill for a long time, and it was a blessing when she finally left me. And it meant she didn't have to see this blasted war.'

'She was very kind to me.'

'She missed you when you left. Looking after your cottage and garden, and your cat filled in my days when Mrs Jenkins passed away.'

'I'd forgotten about Puss. I suppose she—'

'Yes, she is buried at the back of your garden.'

'I didn't even get to say goodbye to you both, did I?' Alice frowned as she tried to remember the day they left. 'And you must tell me what is owed to you.'

'Your father has paid me well over the years.' As he waved a gnarled and spotted hand, Alice knew he must be into his eighties by now. 'It is enough for me now to have you back next door. You left very suddenly, but we understood. And it was probably for the best.'

'Understood what? Why did we have to leave? My father had a good job in Frome, and we had a happy life in the cottage. And I so loved going to the school in the village. I had friends there.' She looked past him through the window out to the fields behind his cottage. 'Although Mummy was much happier when we moved to London. We did have a lot of fun there.'

Mr Jenkins looked down at her and his gaze was so intense, Alice began to feel uncomfortable.

'She never told you why she was so desperate to leave?'

'No.' Alice shook her head. 'Do you know why?'

Mr Jenkins turned away and the only thing to be heard for a long while was the rattling of cups. He disappeared into the scullery behind the kitchen and came back with a jug of milk. 'I don't have any sugar for our tea. I've learned to take my tea without it.'

'Oh, I forgot. I brought some cake.' Alice pointed to the package on the table. 'If you could pass me a knife, I'll slice some for us.'

A few minutes later Mr Jenkins sat opposite her. The tea was poured, the cake was sliced, and the silence was heavy.

Alice swallowed and repeated her question. 'Mr Jenkins, do you know why we had to leave so suddenly?'

'You're old enough to know now.' He looked at her over the rim of his mug and his eyes were sad. 'Your mother was frightened by what happened here.'

Alice frowned. 'What happened? Can you tell me what it was that frightened her?'

'She never told you when you grew up?'

'No. We never talked about the cottage once we went to London. There were so many new and wonderful things there, I'm sorry to say I soon forgot our time here.'

'About a year before you left, a young girl from Glastonbury went missing.'

'And that frightened my mother?'

Mr Jenkins nodded. 'Yes, she used to talk to my Beverley about it. She even hated you going to school, because you were out of her sight. When the second child disappeared, she was inconsolable, and began to say some strange things. Beverley was worried about her state of mind.'

'What sort of strange things?' Alice was surprised. She was sure she had been told nothing of missing children.

Mr Jenkins cleared his throat. 'There are many stories about this area, and your mother believed them. Your granny had told her.'

'Stories about what?' Alice frowned again. 'I do remember that Mother hated the stories that Granny used to tell me. About a magical forest and elves and wizards.'

Mr Jenkins chuckled. 'That was your Granny. She had a wonderful imagination.'

Alice put her teacup in the saucer. 'So, what were the stories my mother believed?'

'The village of Glastonbury is supposed to be located on a magical line. And the line crosses the fields behind our cottages on the way to Land's End.'

'A magical line?'

'Yes. She told Beverley that certain historic places in England are sacred, and some people believe that this is because they are linked by straight lines that connect these places, as well as some ancient landmarks.'

'Do you mean like Glastonbury Abbey?' That was the only historic place close by that Alice could think of.

'No, St Michael's Tower on Glastonbury Tor. It is linked to our stones by a direct line and that then continues north to Avebury.'

'Our stones? Where does all this come from and what's it got to do with missing children? I don't understand,' Alice said. She wondered how much Mr Jenkins believed what he was saying; he seemed to know a lot about it rather than simply repeating something his wife had conveyed to him.

'Some believe that the powerful energy of the ley lines creates an entry point into other times.'

'A time gate?' Alice said slowly. She closed her eyes trying to remember where she'd heard that phrase, but the memory stayed elusive. 'Are you saying that it's believed these children disappeared through those entry points into other times?'

'No, although I see some merit in the idea of ley lines—lass, there are many things we are not aware of— I think that talk is a load of codswallop. Your mother was convinced that was where the girls had gone, and she got my Beverley believing it too. Beverley tried to convince me that little Victoria Hoddle had gone through a time gate.'

'I remember now where I heard it!' Alice squeezed her hands together. 'Mummy was sitting at the table crying one day and she said to Daddy that's where I had gone. I was in the cellar, and I hated to hear her crying. We moved to London that same week. I didn't even go back to school.'

Mr Jenkins nodded as he held her gaze. 'She was terrified that you would go wandering and go through the stones like she believed Amelia Adnum had. Then when the second child, Victoria, disappeared, your mother wouldn't let you out of her sight.'

'I remember Amelia. She was in my class at the school. We used to play hopscotch together. I thought that she had moved away. I didn't hear anything about her going missing.' Alice frowned as she tried to remember but she had been too young to take much notice then.

'I don't think they told any of the children what had happened because they didn't want to frighten them,' Mr Jenkins said.

Alice's laugh was bitter. 'A lot less frightening than the daily fear of being killed in your home by a German bomb, I would say. I didn't know about it anyway, but Mother walked me to the village school every day and was there waiting outside for me every afternoon when it was time to come home. And I wasn't allowed to ever leave our garden.'

'It was sensible that she did that. There were a lot of gypsies and tinkers around that summer, and most of the villagers believed that's what happened to those two children.'

'Taken by gypsies?'

'That is where they would have gone, poor mites.' Mr Jenkins nodded, and pushed back his chair. 'I have to go to the village and help out at the hall this morning. There are some children arriving on the train this afternoon from London, and we are allocating them to work in gardens and farms.'

'That's what I've come down here for. To see if the cottage is suitable to bring some children down here to stay with me. I will take the train back to London tomorrow. The quicker I am, the safer they will be.'

'It will be good company for you, lass. I thought about it, but I'm too old and set in my ways. It wouldn't be fair to the children to have to live with a crotchety old man. But I'm happy to help out in the village while I can.'

'You're not a crotchety old man.' Alice stood and took her teacup to the sink. 'Thank you for the tea, and the kind welcome. I think I'm going to be very happy here. Even though my parents are gone, it feels as though I've come home.' As she turned to leave, she paused. 'Mr Jenkins? What did you mean by *our* stones?

Chapter 7

When Alice went back to Violet Cottage, she opened the downstairs windows to air the musty smell. The cloud had cleared and even though it was cold, the sun was shining from a pale blue sky. She unpacked the rest of the food parcel Maureen had given her and unwrapped the one from the stationmaster. She looked in each of the downstairs cupboards and was pleased to find crockery and saucepans, realising how little thought she had given to her move to the cottage. In the cupboard under the stairs, the smell of mothballs was overpowering but there was enough linen there to make up all the beds once she had aired the sheets and blankets.

In the late morning, with a reluctant sigh, Alice climbed the stairs again. First, she opened the door of the bedroom where she had slept as a child. Unlike downstairs, the room was sparsely furnished. An iron-framed bed, a mattress and a small cupboard filled the space. There was no sign that she had once slept and played and dreamed in this room; all her books and her one doll had gone to London with them.

Reluctantly, she opened the door to her parents' bedroom, but relief filled her as her eyes scanned the dimly-lit room. There were no memories here, and no pangs of sadness came as she stood there. The curtains at the window were pulled shut, but a chink of sunlight lit the room enough to see a double bed, with another single bed tucked in the corner, and a large dressing table against the far wall. Alice crossed to the dressing table, and pulled open a drawer, but it was empty.

She turned to the window and pulled the curtains open. Dust mites danced in the beam of sunlight as she tried to push the window open. The metal catch was stiff, but it finally opened with a loud metallic screech.

Alice drew a deep breath as her eyes scanned the back garden, lifted over the brick wall, now bare of any roses, and settled on the fields beyond. The beech tree was only a hundred yards away, a lot closer than it had appeared to be when she had peered through the gap in the wall that summer evening long ago.

Her breath caught as her gaze moved eastward to three tall stones in the middle of the field.

Our stones, she thought.

The mythical stones that had consumed her mother and made her believe that two young girls had disappeared because of them.

Alice shook her head. As much as she had missed living in the country, it had been a wise move for them to move to London. Her mother's sanity had obviously been at risk.

She stood straight and pulled the curtains open wide to let more sunlight in to air the room where she had decided she would sleep. There was no time to daydream; she had work to do. She would get Mr Jenkins to help her move the single bed into the other bedroom when she came back from London with the children. Between the two single beds and the sofa downstairs, she could take three children.

Now that she had made a mental list of what was in the cottage, it was time to make a shopping list and find the village.

Alice had been surprised to find that the tiny closet beside the front door still held coats and gumboots. She guessed that they hadn't been needed in the city and she did remember that Mummy had bought her a new red coat the first winter they had lived in London. She smiled as she pulled out the navy blue coat that she had worn to the village school in winter. It would be suitable for one of the children she would take in. Rummaging deeper, she pulled out an emerald green cloak that she remembered her mother wearing when she had walked her to school. Alice slipped it around her shoulders and her eyes misted as she imagined she caught a faint trace of her mother's rose perfume, but it was soon gone.

It was a much warmer garment than the coat she had been given at the evacuation centre and she would wear it into the village. The road would be muddy from the melted snow, and she examined the three pairs of gumboots that were at the back of the closet. One pair were about the right size, and she pulled them on after checking inside for spiders.

Alice collected her purse, her notepad and her pencil, and put them in the deep pocket of the cloak along with a handkerchief. She locked the door behind her, placing the key back under the cobblestone in the corner.

Mr Jenkins' door was closed and there was no sign of Cyril; they must still be in the village. Alice had intended to ask Mr Jenkins the best direction to walk to the shop, but they had talked more about the missing children and the mysterious stones. From memory—which could be very wrong—Alice thought it would be quicker to walk along the road to get to Pilton village, but she was sure that Glastonbury was closer if she cut across the fields. There would be more chance of a shop being open in the larger town.

Excitement filled her as she walked up the side of Mr Jenkins' cottage and into his back garden, past the winter vegetable beds and to the wooden gate in the back fence on the side next to the brick wall of her cottage.

My cottage. The words rolled around on her tongue. She was feeling a lot more settled and happier since she had arrived, and she would go up to London when she had prepared the cottage for some children to stay with her.

At the gate a well-trodden path met her, and she knew if she followed it she would end up in the village or the town. As long as there was a store where she could purchase some basics, and ask about the delivery of milk and meat, it didn't matter where she ended up. She had enough money in her purse to start a shop account and was looking forward to meeting some of the locals. She wondered if she would remember any of her schoolfriends, if indeed they still lived here.

The path was high and surprisingly dry considering it had snowed last night. As she headed across the field, Alice looked up. The sun was high in the sky, and she estimated it was close to midday; perhaps she would have some lunch in the village. The path headed west, and she knew then she was right; it must lead to Glastonbury. A cow mooed close to her and she looked nervously across to the small herd in the middle of the field. As she walked on, a faint humming sound filled the air and she paused with a frown. It sounded like a swarm of bumble bees, but as she looked around there were no insects to be seen.

She had almost reached the stone markers and as she walked towards the large one on the left the buzzing became louder, and she kept her eyes wide, not wanting to walk into a swarm of bees. They must be building a hive on the other side of the stone. Alice frowned. No. it was winter. She knew enough about country life to know there would be no bees, the queen hibernated in winter and the rest of the hive died off.

What was that strange sound? If she closed her eyes, she could almost hear music beneath the buzzing. Perhaps there was a pipe band in the village?

The largest blue stone loomed in front of Alice, so close she could almost reach out and touch it. It was much larger than it had looked from the window of the cottage. The piece of stone stood at waist height and she reached out to touch the hard surface. As her fingers touched the warm stone, a bright shaft of light shot from the top towards the sun, bathing her in a blue light and she pulled her hand back quickly. But the swift movement brought her off balance and her gum boot twisted beneath her in a small indentation in the soft ground.

Reaching out to save herself from falling, both hands landed flat against the edge of the huge rock and Alice gasped as the now-cold stone bit into her skin. Panic swirled inside her as the light faded and the landscape around her turned into night as the humming noise became deafening.

She fell to her knees and her forehead touched the rock. Cold sliced through her skin and gripped her bones; she felt so weak she could barely breathe. The little bit of light left was almost gone, and Alice pulled herself up to her feet. The rock was moving, shimmering and shining beside her, but strangely everything was still in darkness. She focused on the rock, trying desperately to see.

It's the grief, she told herself. *And I'm overtired from sleeping on the sofa last night. I need to go back to the cottage and rest.* The grief of losing Mother and Daddy. A delayed reaction to the events of the past months, that's all it was. It was a waking dream.

A strange feeling filled her, as though her bones and muscles had no substance. The pain had gone but now worry took hold of her fleeting thoughts. If she passed out, no one would know who she was. She put her hand in the cloak pocket, feeling for her purse. If she was found in the field, no one would know she came from Violet Cottage. The address in her purse was still the flat in London. Her notebook had nothing in it but dates and diary entries.

They could even think she was a German spy.

I'll be all right. Fight it. Breathe through it.

It was as though her body was weakening more with every breath yet stretching at the same time. Alice fought the weakness that was overtaking her limbs and suddenly her airways relaxed, and as she inhaled, she pitched forward onto the cold, damp ground.

Chapter 8

The happy trill of a bird woke Alice from her faint. She was surprised to find herself sitting up with her back to the rock; she had no recollection of getting to that position. Using one hand to balance herself against the rock, she stood there for a moment wondering whether to go back to the cottage and rest or continue to the village.

As she stood there, her head cleared and the faintness receded completely, and she decided to go on, but to walk slowly. The air was bitterly cold and there were more clouds than there had been when she had set out and it seemed much later in the day. She wrapped Mother's cloak tightly around herself and began to walk. After a few minutes, her body warmed as the sun came out again. Ahead she could hear children's voices, and relief ran through her. She must be getting close to the town.

There was a slight hill ahead, and Alice's leg muscles pulled tight as she climbed to the top. The gum boots were a little large for her and were difficult to walk in. She looked up as the voices became louder and she recognised the nursery rhyme from her childhood.

Three children were running around on the crest —a tall boy and girl, and a smaller boy—chanting the words over and over. The words of *'Baa baa black sheep, have you any wool'* drifted down to her.

'My uncle's sheep have more wool than yours,' the tallest girl called out, a nasty tone to her words.

Alice stopped as a bit of rough jostling began.

'He has not, Amelia,' the little boy said sticking his foot out, so the older girl tripped over. 'Besides, Lord Branton has the most sheep in the district and my father says he is going to take some of his sheep because the wool is secret.'

'You talk foolish talk, Johnny Jenkins.'

The three children went running down the other side of the hill, and for the first time Alice noticed that they were in costume.

Jenkins? That must be a coincidence She knew that Mr and Mrs Jenkins had had no children, and no family in Somerset.

Setting off in the direction that the children had taken, and hoping it would take her to Glastonbury, she put her head down, watching where she placed her feet as the ground was quite boggy. She shivered as a slight wave of dizziness caused her to stumble.

Eventually she came to a stone fence, and when she could see no gate, she held her cloak high and climbed over it. As she walked along the other side of the fence she looked up and was pleased to see Glastonbury Tor not far away.

Alice took a sharp breath and then stopped dead; she must have taken a wrong path. It wasn't Glastonbury Tor because there were no tower ruins on the hill ahead of her. A whole church with towers intact and spires reaching to the sky sat atop the hill. She could even see the sunlight glinting on the stained glass windows.

Lifting her shoulders in a shrug, Alice set off again. It could be any one of several villages; this was a populous part of Somerset and her knowledge of which villages surrounded her cottage was minimal. If she found a village store to buy the staples she needed and had something to eat before she made her way back to the cottage, it didn't matter which village she found.

If she could remember the way back to the cottage. If she couldn't, she would ask the way home. All of a sudden, Alice felt foolish. How irresponsible had she been to head off alone with no idea of where she was going. She should have waited to ask Mr Jenkins.

A niggle of unease prickled her neck as Alice kept walking. Something felt wrong, but she couldn't put a name to the strange feeling that gripped her.

Suddenly there was a loud sound ahead and she dropped to the ground instinctively. It had sounded like a small explosion.

Oh, God. More bombs. She closed her eyes and put her hands over her head, waiting for the next one to fall.

But there was a long silence, and she lifted her head and looked up curiously; there was no sound or sight of a plane overhead.

Smoke drifted across the sky above a forest a short distance to the east, and as she sat there the sounds of men yelling reached her. Looking around for somewhere to hide, she realised she was exposed in the open and there was nowhere to hide.

As she stood considering what to do, thundering hooves came from behind and before she could run, a huge horse was beside her, stamping its hooves and snorting.

A man in a dark cloak leaned down and held out both hands. 'Quickly, mistress. It's not safe. Take my hands.'

Without hesitation, she took the proffered hands and was swung up onto the back of the massive animal.

The man placed Alice in front of him and as the smell of horse, sweat and leather surrounded her she tried not to breathe in too deeply. The world spun and hooves thudded on the turf below as the horse galloped away from the forest.

Alice was terrified; she had never been on a horse before and the sight of the ground rushing past beneath them made her even dizzier than she had been before. The man's arms were around her and she looked around frantically but there was nothing to hang on to as the horse leaped up a steep hill. Feeling helpless, she gripped the hands that held the reins in front of her and held on for grim death.

A small stand of trees was ahead and once they were under cover, the creature slowed, and the world stopped tilting. Maybe it had been her earlier dizziness that had made the ride so frightening. The light in the woods was dim and despite being grateful to the man for removing her from danger, she wondered who he was, and whether she had put herself in a different sort of danger.

She twisted around and looked up. His attention was focused on the woods surrounding them, but after a moment he must have realised she had turned.

'Are you all right, mistress?' he asked.

'I am, thank you,' she said quietly. 'I am happy for you to let me off now. I can't hear a plane anymore.' Alice frowned. 'I actually didn't hear one at all. Do you not have warning sirens in the country?'

His expression was hard to read as he looked down at her. 'I will take you to the town. I assume that is where you are from. Glastonbury? Do you not know it is unsafe to be walking out in the fields these days? If you had stayed on the path, it would be safer.'

'I think it is a lot safer than London.'

'That may be, but there is still danger for a woman to be near the forest.'

'There is danger for everyone, not just women,' she said thinking of her father, killed on his way home from work. 'I'll be fine, now. If you would kindly let me down, I will continue to the village.'

'Which village would that be? I thought you were walking towards Glastonbury town.'

Alice bit her lip. 'I thought I was too, but I felt a little faint and I think I misjudged which way I was going.'

His tone held a hint of impatience. 'You wish to go to Glastonbury? If you are not well, perhaps you should not be out walking.'

'I am perfectly all right now. I need to get to a store, buy some groceries and get back to the cottage before dark.' Alice looked up at the sky; the clouds had come in again and were dark and threatening. 'I don't want to be caught in the snow.'

'There is no chance of snow,' he replied. 'And there is no *grossier* in town. Unless you are seeking a wool merchant.'

This fellow was really annoying her, but she held back her temper. 'It snowed last night when I arrived, and the clouds look dark enough now that it may snow again.'

'Mistress, are you sure you have not had too much sun? It did not snow last night. It has not snowed for many weeks.'

'I beg your pardon, but it certainly did.' If she had been standing, Alice would have stamped her foot. 'Now let me down and let me find my way to town. You didn't answer my question. Are there warning sirens in the country?'

'A warning siren?' He looked at her quizzically.

Before she could reply he had let her go and was off the horse and on the ground in one swift movement. Alice clung to the raised leather thing in front of her and tried not to slip off the horse.

'Let go of the pommel.' Strong hands reached up and encircled her waist, and before she could blink, she was on the ground beside him.

He did not remove his hands and she stared up at him; he was tall and a fine-looking man. Black hair framed dark blue eyes set in a pleasant face. His cloak had slipped over his back and broad shoulders filled a rough wool shirt. She frowned as her eyes travelled down to his feet. He was wearing tight leather breeches and strange soft boots that were laced to his knees. The black cloak hung from his shoulders and covered his back. He was in costume the same as the children had been.

Relief filled her. 'Is there a festival or a re-creation on today? I saw children in costume like yours.'

'The harvest festival?' Concern etched his fine features as he frowned down at her. 'I think perhaps I need to take you somewhere safe.'

Her neck prickled again, and she took a step back. 'If you would direct me to a village where I can buy some food, I will be on my way.'

Her breath caught as he reached out and held both her arms in a firm grip. 'No, I cannot do that. I will take you to my manor, and when I am sure you are well and remain safe, I will take you to Glastonbury myself.'

'Your manor?'

'Yes.'

'Who are you?'

'My deepest apologies, mistress.' He let go of her arms and bowed to her. 'I am Lord Branton of Brue Manor. And may I ask who you are?'

'I am Alice McLaren and I have just moved to Violet Cottage.'

'I am not familiar with that cottage. Does your husband work as a farmhand for Jenkins? Or does he work at the fulling mill? My man, Davies, told me a new family had come to the estate.'

His language was strange and an icy cold ran from Alice's chest up into her throat, and when she tried to speak, words would not come. Finally, she cleared her throat and managed to speak, keeping her voice firm. 'How far is it to Glastonbury from your manor?'

'No more than a mile.'

'Perhaps I could have a cold drink there and then I will go to town.' Her head was spinning, and she was worried she was going to faint again. 'I apologise if I seem vague, but I took the train down from London last night and I had to sleep on the sofa as there was no light in the cottage.'

'Come.' He turned to the horse, after giving her another strange look.

'I'm not getting back on that horse. I will walk behind you.' At least that way she would have some control of where she went. If needs be, she would go on alone, but the way she was feeling, Alice was worried that she would not be able to get to the village herself.

'Very well. I am not leaving you here for a vagrant to apprehend you. I shall walk with you.' His voice was kind but held concern. 'When I say it is not safe, I am telling you what is truth.'

Again, that strange inflection to his words, but Alice nodded.

'Thank you.'

Lord Branton of Brue Manor, as he had called himself, took the reins with one hand and crooked his elbow, looking at her quizzically. Alice hesitated and then slipped her arm through his.

Chapter 9

Branton - 19th April 1496

Branton was surprised when the young woman willingly put her arm through the crook of his elbow and allowed him to lead her through the woods. They were not far from the entrance to his manor, but he was concerned about her health, she was talking strangely and using words that he had not heard before.

She walked beside him and kept hold of his arm as he led the horse up the hill. When they reached the crest, he looked across his fields with satisfaction. From the crest of this hill you could see all his land, and as far as the town. As he looked out over the green fields dotted with his sheep, the voices of children carried up the hill to them.

'There!' The young woman called Alice pointed. 'Those are the children I saw in costume.'

Branton shook his head and spoke gently. 'Yes, they are some of the local tenants' children. I let them play in the fields as long as they don't disturb the sheep.'

He let the reins go and slapped the horse on the rump. 'Home, Black. I'll see to you in a while.'

His stallion snorted and broke into a canter along the familiar path towards the stables.

'Will he know where to go?' Her voice held concern.

'Yes, don't worry, he knows the way home and he will be keen to get to the bag of oats he knows will be waiting for him.' Branton swept his arm in a circle as he spoke to the young woman. 'It's not far distant. There is Brue Manor ahead—it is not far for us to walk from here. My land goes from the River Brue in the west'—he turned, and she turned with him as he pointed to the east— 'to the forest behind the three marker stones on the eastern boundary.'

As he pointed, Alice followed the direction he was pointing in.

'Where . . . where . . . where are the cottages?' The pitch of her voice rose, and her fingers gripped his other arm so tightly, he could feel the coldness of her fingers through the wool of his shirt. 'I cannot see the cottages, and they should be over there.'

He kept looking east. The marker stones were clearly defined against the dark green of the Brue forest behind them. The river wound along the other side of the forest. It was one of Branton's favourite places to ride and sit by the water when he needed to think. He'd been doing a lot of that lately, as he tried to figure out who was stealing his sheep.

'What cottages do you refer to?' he asked.

'The other side of the three stones. The stones are between our two cottages and Glastonbury. It was there that I felt ill and I think I fainted. I had only come a short distance from the stones when I heard that bang, and then I saw the children and then you picked me up onto your horse. Where am I? Where have the cottages gone? I need to go and look now. Right now.' Distress filled her voice and Branton felt sympathy for the poor woman.

'There are ten cottages on my land for my tenants, but they are situated on the other side of the hill closer to Glastonbury, near the water mills. There are no cottages near the stones and there never have been.'

'But Violet Cottage and Mr Jenkins' Rose Cottage should be over there. There is a forest there now and the beech tree has gone. I may not know the area, but I could see Glastonbury Tor with the ruined tower on the top from the upstairs window. I am in the right place.' Her eyes were wide, and her voice was becoming frantic. 'Where is my cottage? It must be on the other side of the stones. I can't see it, or Mr Jenkins cottage.'

'There are no cottages to the east. I have lived here for all of my thirty years and have never seen a cottage there.' Branton's concern grew. There was something not quite right with this woman. 'Do you think you are able to walk a short distance, or shall I carry you? Did you hit your head when you fell?'

'No. Well, perhaps a little. But I don't have a head injury or a headache.' Despite her words she let go of him and pressed her fingers to her temples. She held her head as she turned it from side to side. 'I must be dreaming. This must be a dream. Perhaps I am still in London and didn't even come down here. Mother was right. Maybe I shouldn't have come to Somerset.'

Branton took her hands and tried to soothe her distress. 'Mistress, I can assure you this is not a dream. You are in Somerset.' He smiled at her. 'But please be assured I will take care of you, until you feel well again. Please take my arm and we will go and sit down and let you partake of some refreshment and rest for a while. Then everything will seem all right once more.' Concern filled Branton as he looked down at her. Her face was chalk white, and her eyes were wide. She lifted a shaking finger and pointed to the church on the hill on the Tor. 'Is that . . . is that St Michael's church?'

He nodded. 'It is. A new church was built there a hundred years ago to replace the one that was damaged in the earthquake. It is a part of the monastery there. A daughter house of our abbey.'

'What earthquake?' she asked.

'The one over two hundred years ago.'

'Oh my God.' Her swift intake of breath left her face even whiter. 'Tell me' She tugged at his arm. 'That noise that I heard. The smoke. Tell me what it was. Please.' Her eyes beseeched him to be truthful.

'There has been some local unrest since our king asked parliament to sanction subsidies and to increase the taxes. There are many who do not agree, and that is why I was fearful of your safety. There has been some unrest, but I heard no noise.' Branton suspected the noise she had heard had something to do with those stealing his sheep, but he did not voice that thought. She could even be a decoy to take him away while the sheep were herded in the other direction.

'It wasn't a bomb, then that I heard?' She looked up. 'From the sky?'

He shook his head slowly. 'I am unsure of what you ask. The noise that you heard could have been corned powder. When combined with fire, it will make a loud noise and smoke. Things in the country are uncertain and can be unsafe at the moment. That is why I was concerned to see you wandering in the forest without an escort.'

Her shoulders slumped and Branton was distressed to hear a sob break from her lips. She grabbed at his hands and her eyes held his.

'Please tell me where I am.' Her head shook from side to side and her cloak slipped from her shoulders to reveal clothes different to any he had seen the likes of before.

As he reached down and placed the cloak back around her shoulders, her expression tore at his heart. She looked lost and frightened.

'You are on my estate in Somerset, a mile from Glastonbury. Please be calm, mistress, and I will take you to my manor. My housekeeper will take care of you. And we will make sure you are well again before you continue your journey.'

He was pleased that she remained quiet as he led her down the hill and through the stone pillars at the gates of the manor.

***

Alice

Alice looked down at the boggy ground as she trudged beside her rescuer—that was how she now regarded him—and Mr Jenkins' words, and those of her mother, circled around and around in her head.

Ley lines. Powerful energy. Time gate. An entry to another world.

There was no other explanation; she knew now that she was not dreaming. The landscape was sharply defined and detailed; she could smell the wet earth beneath her feet, the wet wool of Lord Branton's shirt, and she could hear sheep bleating in the fields around them.

The man beside her was very real. None of what she was experiencing was a dream and had nothing to do with a head injury or her faint.

It was the stones. She knew that deep inside her, and she knew it to be the truth. All she had to do now was accept that she had gone through into a different time and she had to figure out what she was going to do.

No one would miss her. Maureen and the rest of the workers at the evacuation centre thought she was in Somerset, and Mr Jenkins would assume that she had taken the train back to London and decided to stay there. Alice drew a deep breath. As long as she was safe here—and it had to be safer here than being in the midst of the war—she would calm down and make the best of the strange situation she had found herself in.

Alice focused on her breathing.

In and out.

In and hold.

In and out.

I must remain calm.

Lord Branton slowed his step and Alice looked up, drawing in another deep breath at the sight of the house ahead. She held it in as her eyes scanned the beautiful building in front of them. It was more than a house—he had called it his manor. The manor house on his estate, and that was exactly how she would describe the building she was looking at. The bricks glowed a soft honey colour in the afternoon sun. Surrounded by colourful gardens as far as she could see at the front and at each side, it was almost like one of her mother's favourite jigsaw puzzles. As Alice's eyes roamed the beautiful scene, she spotted a figure standing at the side of one of the lead lighted windows on the upper storey.

'Welcome to Brue Manor, Mistress Alice.' His voice was deep and melodious, but most of all it was kind.

'Thank you, Lord Branton.' She kept her voice respectful. 'May I ask you one more thing. It may seem like a strange question, but please humour me. Would you tell me what year and month we are in?'

She looked up and his dark eyes held hers, and she found it hard to look away. His expression was calm, and it helped soothe her.

'It is April, in the year of our Lord 1496.'

Alice reached out and gripped his forearms, unable to stop the soft cry of distress that burst from lips.

She was right. No matter how strange it was, she had travelled to 1496. Sickness roiled in her stomach and she tried desperately to ground herself.

Even though she had accepted what had happened and that somehow she had stumbled through a time gate, it was still hard to hear those words.

It was April, 1496.

Her suspicions were right. She had found the time gate that she had heard her mother speak of all those years ago, and the theory of entering another time that Mr Jenkins had espoused but had not believed was true.

Chapter 10

Mistress Oatley, the housekeeper at Brue Manor, had come as soon as Lord Branton had summoned her, and she looked at Alice curiously as they waited in silence for him to return. He had explained that his guest was unwell and would be resting at the manor for a short time. The tall woman stood at the door and did not acknowledge Alice's presence after he'd left the room.

Alice didn't know if it was normal behaviour for the time or of it was merely rudeness that had put the morose expression on Mistress Oatley's face.

'Would you please bring some blackberry wine and some bread and figs,' Branton requested when he came back into the room. He had shed his cloak, and obviously washed, as the dark curls around his face were now damp.

'Yes, my lord.'

He had led Alice into a large room at the front of the house and ensured that she was comfortable before he disappeared. She was finding it hard to stay calm and didn't know what to say or do, not wanting to give away that she had no idea how to behave.

Taking a deep breath, she looked around. The walls were richly panelled with dark timber and the long narrow windows of lead-lighted glass had coloured images filling each space. The few pieces of furniture in the room were made of timber and were austere.

Closing her eyes, Alice tried to focus on her dilemma.

What should I do?

Should she tell this man what had happened, or would he think she was mad? No wonder he'd looked at her strangely when she'd asked about bombs, and planes, and said she had taken the train down.

Alice couldn't help the giggle that broke from her lips. He'd probably had visions of her on a camel train. Or did they not know about them either in . . . what was it? The fifteenth century.

Oh my God. The fifteenth century. Was she really there . . . or here? It was hard to know what to think and finding the right words to say was even harder.

Finally, when the long silence became uncomfortable Alice looked up. Lord Branton was sitting in a chair opposite her and she was surprised to see a smile on his face.

'It was good to hear you laugh. You must be feeling better,' he said.

She pulled the edges of her cloak together and nodded. 'I am. I am coming to accept my situation.'

'Your situation?'

'Yes. You were right. I am lost. I am a long way from my home and I—' she fumbled with her cloak as she tried to think of the right words— 'I will need somewhere to stay. The problem is I have no money to pay for. . . for lodging. If I was to go to the Abbey would they take a stranger in?'

'No, I don't think they would take a lone woman. You are—'

He broke off as Mistress Oatley came in with a wooden tray and placed it on the table near the window. She lifted a jug and poured a dark purple liquid into a metal cup. Alice's nostrils twitched; she could smell the sweetness of the blackberries as the liquid was poured. The housekeeper lifted the cup and passed it to Alice.

'Thank you,' she said quietly and lifted it slowly to her lips. Taking a small sip, Alice hesitated as the pungent sweetness exploded on her tongue, and she wondered how alcoholic the concoction was. But nevertheless, it was palatable, and it quenched her thirst. She took another deeper drink. The liquid warmed her throat and she could feel heat rising in her cheeks.

'Would you please ensure that the green room is aired, and that a warming pan is heated for the bed.

Mistress Alice will break her journey here and stay with us.'

Alice's eyes widened in surprise as he gave the instruction. The housekeeper nodded and left the room silently.

'Thank you. You have no reason to be kind to me,' she said.

He leaned forward and his gaze was intense. 'Oh, but I do. You fascinate me. With your strange words, your different attire and your claim to being lost. I could not in good faith let you leave and wander the countryside again. It would not be safe. Once I establish where you wish to go, I will assist you on your journey, but in the meantime, you are welcome to rest in my manor.'

'Why would it not be safe? Surely it is safer in the country or am I being naive?' The more time Alice spent with this man, the more she trusted him. He had done nothing apart from show concern for her well-being.

She leaned back against the hard wooden chair and let her gaze travel over Lord Branton as he reached out and took a dried fig from the tray.

In contrast to his dark hair, his skin was fair, and his eyes a deep cornflower blue.

An unfamiliar quiver tugged at Alice. She frowned. It was the first time she had ever experienced that feeling. Her interactions with male friends in London had been merely an occasional chaste kiss after attending the theatre before the war, but she had never felt this strange, but pleasurable quiver before.

'It is never safe; there are always thieves and brigands around. More so now that many tenant farmers have been removed from their farms. As well as that, recently there have been some strange happenings close by.'

'Strange happenings?' Alice asked quietly. She could relate to that, she thought. More than he would ever know.

'I have been dealing with a dispute between two of the tenant farmers. There have been some unexplained happenings at night. Three of my sheep have disappeared along with one of my shepherds.'

'Where was that?' Her eyes widened. 'Were they near the stones?'

'That is a strange thing to ask.' He raised his eyebrows. 'But no, they were in the home field close to the house. They were a new breed of sheep that I purchased at the market.' He looked across at her and gave her a wide smile as he held her eyes with his. 'From the wool *grossier.*'

Again, that unfamiliar quiver tugged in her lower belly.

'I don't think that would make my journey unsafe, would it?' She smiled back at him. 'I am not at all interested in sheep. I know nothing about them. I have lived in London for most of my life. Although I was born in the cottage across the fields.'

The cottage that doesn't exist yet, to parents who have not yet been born. As the thought came into Alice's mind, a tendril of hope began to weave through her thoughts.

If she could get back to the cottage *before* 1941, perhaps she could change what had happened to her parents. She could go back to London and warn them. But how could she find out how to go back to her time? Let alone decide when she would return. If only she'd had time to find out more about the ley lines before she had gone near the stones. But like Mr Jenkins, she had thought it was a story with no substance.

A wave of grief rolled through Alice. She couldn't believe she hadn't thought of her parents for the past two hours. She looked around. Apart from an elderly man in the garden as they had walked up from the gate, she had not seen anyone else.

Apart from the figure at the window.

'Who else lives here with you? Do you have a wife?' she asked holding his eyes with hers. A strange feeling shimmied through her. It was as if she could read his thoughts, and an intense longing came from deep within. It was hard to look away as Lord

Branton's blue eyes held hers, but she forced herself to look down.

Heat ran up Alice's neck and into her cheeks. She had spent too much time over the past two years reading. Now she was imagining she knew what he was feeling. Not to mention, she now wondered if he had a mad wife locked in the attic.

'Jane Eyre,' she muttered. 'Or Rebecca?'

'No, I do not have a wife,' he said. 'I live here alone, and Mistress Oatley looks after the manor, Mrs Hodges is my cook, and Mr Hodges looks after the garden. I have—or I had—three shepherds who look after my flock, and a stable boy who attends to my horses. And to answer your question, I live alone apart from Mistress Oatley who lives in the house, and the Hodges in a cottage in the back garden behind the stables. Peterkin lives in the village. His father is one of my mill workers.'

'You are young to have a manor house.' She frowned. 'And a title? Lord, you said to me in the woods. And Mistress Oatley, called you "my lord".'

'You are correct. My father was elderly when I was born. He died when I was twenty years of age, and I became the lord of Brue Manor. I have no title as you call it, but I am the lord of my manor, and this estate.'

'It is very hard when you lose a parent.' Alice tried to keep her voice even, as the grief rose. *It is unbearable when you lose both within days of each other*, she thought.

The one blessing was that her mother would never know that her greatest fear had been realised. Alice was no longer a little girl seeking to explore the magical world behind the cottage, but as a grown woman she had accidentally discovered the time gate.

Now she had to figure out how to get back.

Chapter 11
Branton

Mistress Oatley had taken Alice up to her room, and as he sat drinking a tankard of mead, Branton reflected on the strange events of the day. Alice was not familiar to him, and her speech and her words were strange; she did not seem to fit. There was a strangeness about her that he found hard to reconcile with the local women he knew. He recalled a similar incident a few years when a young girl child had been taken in by the Davies. She was lost and didn't know how to get home.

Like Alice, the girl's accent had been slightly different, and her style of dress and shoes had been strange. Few in the district knew of her circumstances, but Robert Davies had asked to speak to Branton when he and his wife, Elizabeth, had taken Amelia in.

The smell of roasting meat drew Branton to the kitchen just before dark. There had been no sign of his guest and Mistress Hodges queried him as he walked into the hall that led to the back of the manor.

'Dinner for you only, my lord?' she asked.

'I'm not sure, Mistress Hodges. Can you please ask Mistress Oatley to go upstairs and check on our guest while I'm in the stables? I want to check that all is secure for the night.'

'Very well, my lord.'

'Would you also ask her to find some of my sister's clothing and shoes for our guest. She . . . ah . . . was not expecting to stay and has brought nothing with her.'

'Yes, my lord.'

As luck would have it, Robert Davies was in the stables shoeing a lame horse that Branton had asked him to attend to earlier that day.

'My lord,' Robert said.

Branton reached into the sack for a carrot and walked over to his stallion. 'Thank you for putting Black in the stable for me.'

'I have heard that you walked home with an unexpected guest.' Davies sent him a curious glance. Despite the difference in their social standing, Branton respected this man; he was a good worker and skilled with the horses. They had worked together on the estate since Branton's father had passed. A friendship had sprung up between them.

'Hodges?'

'Hodges.' Robert smiled and nodded as he turned back to the palfrey. 'Come and hold her steady for me.'

'He has eyes like a hawk that man.'

Black snickered as he took the carrot from his master's hand, and Branton crossed to where Robert was working. 'But his wife is an excellent cook, and he looks after the gardens, so I will not complain.'

'After recent events, I would say you should be pleased to have a gardener who is most observant.'

Branton shook his head. 'Yes, but he saw nothing of the missing sheep or of young Pitkin before he disappeared. Rob, I need to talk to you.'

Robert nailed the hoof into place and stood, looking curiously at Branton, a hint of wariness in his expression.

Branton lifted his hands. 'Don't look at me like that. You should know you have my loyalty and I would never let you go, no matter how much taxes rise. I want to talk to you about Amelia.'

Robert's eyebrows rose. 'Amelia? I thought you were going to say Isabelle. If you intend to ask my sister to be your wife, I am the one you must ask for her hand.'

'I am aware of that for when—if—the time comes.'

'And when will it come, Branton? She is getting impatient and the sheriff would have her as his wife tomorrow.'

Branton pursed his lips; he did not have to explain himself to anyone—even his friend.

'I was asking about Amelia.'

Robert lowered his gaze, obviously realising he wasn't going to get anywhere on his sister's behalf.

Branton had been considering taking Isabelle Davies as his wife. She lived with Robert and his wife in the farmhouse on the outskirts of Mill Village. He still carried guilt from May Day last year when he had been in his cups and had spent time with her in a haystack at the back of the stables.

The right thing to do would be to marry her. She was a fine-looking woman, a lady, an excellent seamstress by all accounts, and she looked at him with those huge pale blue eyes whenever he went across to Robert's farmhouse.

'What did you want to know?' Robert interrupted his thoughts.

'Has Amelia settled in more? Has she stopped that foolish talk of being lost?'

Robert nodded as they walked outside and sat on the low stone wall behind the stables. Mr Hodges was silhouetted in the doorway of the cottage and nodded and turned away when he saw that it was Branton and Robert sitting on the wall.

'Yes, she is fitting in with the other children and seems to have accepted that this is now her home. I still believe she ran away from another farm or village, but we've had no word of anyone looking for a young girl.'

Branton lowered his voice. 'Tell me again what she said about the stones. I didn't pay much attention to it when you first told me.'

Robert sighed and leaned back against the low wall. The sun had set, and the sky was streaked with purple. An owl hooted from the beech tree at the side of the stone wall, and a shiver ran down Branton's back. He didn't believe in superstitions, but the omen of death still made him uneasy.

In the distance the three stones loomed ominously, the thick forest providing a dark dramatic background for the three monoliths.

'Amelia doesn't talk about it now, because, I suppose, no one ever put much credence in what she said. Plus, Elizabeth wouldn't let her go out to be with the other children if she talked about it, but Amelia swore on the Bible that she was telling the truth. I wonder at times, because I know the stories I used to hear about the stones when I was a child. We weren't game to go near them. Old Granny Irvine in the village had all the stories of the stones.'

Branton looked at him steadily for a few moments. 'I was always scared of Granny Irvine when I was a boy. She had the strangest piercing pale white eyes and was always wandering around our fields, no matter that my father told her she was not welcome. What stories did you hear? I recall a few.'

Robert folded his arms and leaned back, ready to settle in. 'Old Granny would disappear for months at a time, and when she'd come back to the village, she was full of stories about the stones. Supposedly the stones were a witch and her two daughters. The three women were set in stone one night because they were there in the dark of the moon. Legend had it that if a young woman went there during an eclipse, she would hear the name of the man she would marry. If a man went there, it was at his own risk. When I was lad, I was the same as you, my brothers and I were terrified to go near them. What did you hear?' Robert asked with a furtive look over his shoulder.

'Much the same. Witchcraft, another about the devil turning three sisters to stone. I've been curious over the years, but each time I go there, something seems to hold me back. What did Amelia say?'

Robert looked around again and made sure Mr Hodges was not in earshot. 'Don't tell Elizabeth I paid heed to the child, but I did. Amelia says she came from a time in the future and that when she touched the stones one afternoon, there was a bright blue light shooting up into the sky and she woke up here. She's not a bad child; she helps Elizabeth with the cooking and with the young ones, but many nights we hear her crying and saying she wants to go home. We've offered to take her back to wherever she ran away from but that makes her cry all the harder.'

'Strange.' Branton shook his head. 'Thanks, for shoeing Bonnie, Robert. I'd best go into the manor in case my guest has come down to dine.' He chuckled. 'Speaking of witches, between you and me, the poor young woman wouldn't be able to cope with Mistress Oatley and Mistress Hodges at the same time.'

'Have a good night, my lord.' Robert smiled and stood. 'I'll see you in the morn. Ah, and Isabelle will be coming over to the manor house to see Mistress Oatley.'

Branton raised his eyebrows. 'Will she? For what reason?'

Robert shrugged. 'I do not know. She asked me to escort her across in the morn.'

'Very well, I will tell Mistress Oatley. I will not be there. I will be out in the fields.'

'Good evening to you, my lord.'

'And to you, too, Rob.'

Branton was thoughtful as he walked across the cobblestones to the manor.

Chapter 12

Alice woke slowly and lay in the soft bed looking at the ceiling. The room in the cottage seemed bigger than she remembered, and the dark wood lining the walls was unfamiliar. She'd had the strangest dream, a dream that had seemed so real with people she had never met before or indeed even heard of.

She jumped when someone tapped on the door.

Who was in her cottage? She was sure she had locked the door, but the door opened immediately after the knock. Her breath caught and she held herself stiff as a woman walked into her bedroom.

Oh, my goodness. It had been no dream. This was Mistress Oatley, one of the people she thought had been a figment of her fevered imagination.

It was real. Every moment of yesterday had been real.

Her faint in the field, the ride on the horse to the manor house, and the enigmatic and handsome lord who had brought her to his home.

'Good morning, Mistress Alice.' The housekeeper was tall, and Alice was yet to see her smile. 'I have brought you some fresh garments and some slippers for your feet. And a *crespinette* to confine your hair.' Her voice as well as her facial expression was disapproving.

'Thank you,' Alice said quietly as she sat up and stretched her arms above her head. That movement brought another disapproving look, and Alice quickly lowered her arms.

'Once you are dressed, if you would like to break your fast, I will meet you in the dining hall. It is beside the parlour where you sat with Lord Branton when you arrived.'

'Thank—'

Another sniff, and the housekeeper was gone.

She looked around the room. How could she have mistaken it for the cottage? It was nothing like it.

The bed had four timber posts and the walls of the room were panelled in timber squares that replicated the shape of the mullioned windows. On the opposite wall a huge tapestry, richly patterned in blues and golds, hung from the ceiling. She closed her eyes and fought the fear that threatened to rise. She had been strong enough to survive the loss of her parents; she could survive this strange situation. All she had to do was figure out how to get back to 1941.

She had managed to come here; surely it wouldn't be hard to get back? All she had to do was go back to the stones and put her hand on them and hopefully it would be as fast and easy as it had been to come to the fifteenth century.

As the realisation hit her that she was indeed in a time five hundred years before she had been born, her head spun, her mouth dried, and she felt as though she was going to be sick. She looked around for a basin or a toilet and realised where—and when— she was.

Fighting back the nausea, Alice flopped back onto the soft feather pillow and the sweet smell of lavender surrounded her. Closing her eyes, she thought back to the night before; she had been expected to go downstairs to dine with the lord, but when Mistress Oatley had shown her to this room and had left her here, the last thing Alice remembered was sitting on the bed, and smelling the lavender as a wave of weariness had washed over her. She must have fallen back and gone into a very deep sleep.

After a few moments, she began to feel better, but was desperately in need of the bathroom. She climbed out of the bed, surprised to see her skirt and jumper folded neatly on the chair. She had no recollection of taking them off. No wonder the housekeeper had looked mortified when she had sat up and stretched her arms, wearing only her underwear.

***

Branton

Branton left the manor at dawn and saddled Black and rode the fields as far as the perimeter of the estate. He saw nothing untoward and the sheep were where they were supposed to be. There was no one else to be seen, although at one point he did think he heard voices and pulled Black beneath a spreading chestnut tree and waited, but there were no more unusual sounds to be heard.

He left the stallion in the field behind the stable, as he intended riding out again after he had eaten.

And had checked on his guest.

Branton had had a sleepless night. Strangely he had not been able to get Alice from his mind. He had been disappointed when she had not come down again last evening after Mistress Oatley had shown her to the guest room upstairs.

It had taken him a long time to get to sleep, and he had dreamed of her when he had finally slept.

His boots clattered on the cobblestones as he walked past the kitchen gardens and Mr Hodges nodded to him as he walked past.

'Morning, Hodges.'

'Morning, my lord, it's going to be a fine day. A fine day indeed.'

And it was.

Branton was looking forward to getting back onto his horse and spending the day in the fresh air. Yesterday afternoon when he had encountered Alice, he had gone out late after a day in the manor house wrestling with the accounts and trying to reconcile the number of sheep in his records with the number of sheep in the fields. He had spent much time trying to decide if Pitkin, the shepherd who had disappeared, was also responsible for the sheep that were no longer to be found. It was out of character. Pitkin was a simple and honest man who had been loyal to Branton, and his father before him.

There was something afoot; he'd talk to Robert about it when he came to the manor this morning.

Branton stifled a groan, remembering that Isabelle would accompany Robert.

When had his life become so complicated?

That was another decision to be made.

And soon.

It was time he was married and brought a mistress to supervise Brue Manor; Mistress Oatley had risen above her station and had far too many opinions to express. He had delayed too long; there was no one more suitable than Isabelle Davies.

Branton stopped by the well and sluiced his face and neck with the cold water. As he lifted his face to the weak sunlight, voices reached him through the door that led to the kitchen.

'Ah, she is a strange one, there is no doubt of that.' Mrs Hodges sounded indignant. 'Came into my kitchen a while ago, demanding to know where the privy was.'

'She is certainly that, whoever she is,' Mistress Oatley said. 'What did you say?'

'I told her in no uncertain terms, we were no castle, and that she could do what the rest of us did.'

'And what did she do then?'

'She looked at me with that superior manner and disappeared.' Mrs Hodges' laugh was loud. 'Mistress Isabelle is not going to be pleased if the master has brought his paramour here.'

'And a strange paramour at that.'

Branton strode into the scullery where the cook was standing with her arms folded over a puffed-out chest. Her face turned scarlet when Branton stared at her unsmilingly.

'My lord,' she said meekly.

'Do you not have work to do? Both of you,' he said firmly.

'Yes, my lord.' Both women put their heads down and went to sidle out of his sight.

'Wait, where is Mistress Alice?'

Mistress Oatley drew herself straight. 'I believe she is sitting in the rose garden.'

'Has she eaten?

Two head shakes and neither of them met his gaze.

'I was preparing the tray for her but had not finished,' Mistress Hodges said.

'And the sun has almost reached its zenith.' Branton's voice was harsh. 'Perhaps she has left the house because she has not been made to feel welcome. I would have you both remember that she is my guest and will be treated with respect.'

'My lord.' Both women nodded and disappeared quickly.

Branton walked through the parlour, anger stiffening his shoulders. He had always been easy with the workers in the manor; perhaps it was time to be firmer. The double wooden doors at the end of the entrance hall were open, and he hurried outside.

He would not be surprised if Alice had left after the rude treatment she had received from the two women. Branton resolved to speak further to them—and Hodges—later in the day.

The gardens were brilliant with colour; spring had taken hold early this year. He walked past the high brick wall that surrounded the rose gardens and turned into the arbour. Fat rosebuds promised even more colour when the roses came into full bloom. He stood and looked around but could see no sign of Alice. As he was about to turn, he heard a sound from the far corner of the garden.

A frown wrinkled his brow as he drew closer. It sounded like a cry. He approached quietly and was dismayed to see Alice sitting on the damp grass with her back to the wall and her head in her hands. Ragged sobs came from her and he hurried over and dropped to his knees on the damp grass beside her.

'Alice,' Branton said quietly, so as not to startle her.

She didn't appear to hear him, and he spoke again, more loudly this time.

Again, no response.

'Alice?' The third time Branton said her name, he reached out tentatively and touched her arm. The grass was damp beneath his knees and she was still dressed in the same strange clothes he had glimpsed beneath her cloak yesterday.

As soon as he touched her arm, Alice jumped and dropped her hands from her face. Branton was shocked at her raw grief. Her eyes were red-rimmed, and her cheeks were wet with tears. But it was the sad expression and the emptiness in her eyes that filled him with sympathy. Unable to help himself, he reached out and put his arms around her and held her close to his chest. Her hair tickled his face and an unfamiliar fragrance filled his nostrils.

He kept his tone low and soothing. 'I am so sorry that Mistress Hodges and Mistress Oatley were rude to you. I have spoken to them.'

He could feel the warmth of her skin through the soft garment beneath his hands.

Her voice was muffled as her face pressed against his shoulder. 'They did not upset me.'

'But you have not eaten, and you have not been given clothes to wear as I requested.' His fingers brushed against the soft wool of the unusual garment that she wore on the top half of her body. It was pink like the roses that were in bud above them, and Branton knew it was wool, but he had never felt wool so soft, nor seen a colour like that.

'No, it was not them. I came out here to sit in the sun and I began thinking of my plight, and my recent . . . recent loss. I felt sorry for myself and I could not stop my tears.' Her face was still pressed against his shoulder and Branton gently rubbed her back. She was obviously grieving, and he wished he could make it better. He searched for something to say that would help but could think of nothing.

Finally, she lifted her head and pulled away from him and her eyes held his.

'Thank you, you are very kind to me . . . my lord.' There was a deep flush high on her cheeks and her lips were softly parted and a strange feeling ran through Branton. Despite her red and puffy eyes, she was very beautiful. Her dark brown hair fell in soft waves around her face, and her lips were full and lush.

'It distresses me to see you so sad.'

As she sat back, she laid a hand over her heart. 'I am sad as I have no one left in my life. My mother and father were killed a few weeks ago. I suppose because of my plight here, I began to think that no one will miss me and that made me upset.'

Branton couldn't help himself. He wanted to touch her again. He lifted his hand and cupped her cheek.

'*I* will miss you when you go back to your home.'

'I don't know how to get to my home.'

'That is one way I can help you,' he said.

She shook her head and looked at him almost in disbelief, and he remembered the strange words she had used. 'That would be very good,' she said slowly. 'But it is impossible unless—'

Again, she stared at him as though she was trying to probe his thoughts. As her eyes held his, a pleasurable shiver ran down Branton's back and he determined that no matter what she needed, he would assist her.

'I think, Mistress Alice, I need to get to know you better, so I can find a way to help you return to your cottage. Today I am riding the boundaries of my estate. Perhaps you could accompany me, and we can talk of your plight.'

She nodded slowly. 'I would like that. Perhaps I may find a clue to the way home.'

He stood and brushed the damp grass from his breeches, and then held out both his hands to her. She hesitated and then reached out and placed her small soft hands in his. He pulled her up and for a moment the length of her body touched his from head to toe, and an unbidden jolt of desire had the blood rushing downwards from his heart.

'The first thing we shall do is ensure that mistress Oatley finds you some suitable garments.' He held her arm and turned towards the gate.

'She already has.' Her sigh was deep, and she looked resigned. 'But I didn't know how to put the three pieces on. And the head thing she gave me . . .' Her shoulders lifted in a shrug and this time she laughed. 'It totally bamboozled me. I had no idea what to do with it.'

'Bamboozled? I have never heard that word? Have you once lived in France? That would explain your strange accent.' He stepped back to let her go ahead as they reached the gap in the brick wall that surrounded the rose arbour.

'I have visited France, but I have not lived there. I have spent most of my life in London.'

'Ah, so you would have been privy to the doings of the usurper Perkin Warbeck.'

Alice shook her head. 'No. I have not heard of him. I have not—' She bit her lip as though to stop herself saying more, and he wondered for the first time if he was too trusting. Perhaps she had an ulterior motive for being on his land. Perhaps he had been swayed by a beautiful face, and then Branton remembered her tears and genuine grief and confusion.

'Come. We will get you some refreshment, and I will get Mistress Oatley to assist you to dress.'

'Is there somewhere I can wash?' Her cheeks coloured. 'I found the privy outside, but it is very different to what I am used to.'

'You have me intrigued, Mistress Alice. I am looking forward to hearing your story as we ride. I would like to get out into the fields as quickly as we can.'

Branton wanted to be gone before Isabelle arrived to see Mistress Oatley.

Chapter 13

Mistress Oatley must have had a change of heart after the lord had spoken to her. She was a different woman to the dour housekeeper who had shown Alice to the guest room last night. When Alice returned to her room, the housekeeper quickly appeared with a wooden tray laden with fruit and nuts, and a tankard of apple cider, and the woman could not have been more pleasant. As Alice sat on the chair near the window and made herself eat—the last thing she felt like was food, but she knew she needed to keep her strength up—Mistress Oatley reappeared with a jug of warm water and a cloth.

'Perhaps you would let me braid your hair, and then we will be able to put your headpiece on. Once you are dressed, I shall return.' As she reached the door she turned with a smile. 'Put the linen chemise on first and then I will help you with the dress. It is a heavy dress, but it will be warm beneath your cloak. The master told me you are going with him on Black.

You will need your cloak and your head covered. The day has turned cool.'

Alice glanced across to the mullioned window as the woman closed the door behind her. Grey clouds filled the sky, and it looked as though rain threatened. Perhaps they would not ride after all.

Disappointment knifed through her. She knew Lord Branton was genuine, and she wondered how much she should tell him.

Could she trust him?

Would he think she was a fool and send her packing?

Perhaps they could ride to the stones, and she could show him how they vibrated beneath her fingertips.

Fear held Alice in a tense grip. Why had she ended up in 1496? What was so special about this time that she went through the vortex and ended up in the fifteenth century in the same location that she had left? She needed to talk to somebody who knew of these things.

Why, oh why, hadn't she paid more attention to Mr Jenkins when he was talking about ley lines and time gates?

She wondered how much her mother had known. The memory of her mother's fear fed Alice's fear; she must have known there was danger. Perhaps she had experienced it herself? Or perhaps she knew of some who had. Or maybe it was just because of the two children who had disappeared, those that Mr Jenkins had mentioned.

What if she touched the stone and she went to a different time? What if she went somewhere where there was danger? At least she knew where the stones were. She had been very lucky that Lord Branton had come along and rescued her yesterday.

It could have been a lot worse.

With a sigh, she turned to the bed and lifted the rough linen chemise over her head.

As Alice walked down the timber staircase half an hour later after she had been assisted by a still pleasant Mistress Oatley, she tried to get used to the feel of the rough fabric rubbing her skin beneath this borrowed dress, and the confinement of the headpiece that was pulling at the tight coils beneath it. The housekeeper had braided her hair, and then coiled the braids beneath the head band.

When she managed to put the fear and the uncertainty aside, Alice had begun to take a great interest in her surroundings. Physical things were very different: the clothes, the food, the interior of the manor house, the lack of facilities—she dreaded going back to that privy, but she knew she would have to. Despite the different surroundings, people appeared to have the same natures she was used to.

The kindness of Lord Branton and his determination to see her happy reminded her of her father when Mother had been upset. The gossiping and the nastiness of the two women in the house—although that appeared to have been addressed—was no different to some of the volunteers at the evacuation centre.

As she thought of home, another ripple of fear shuddered though her, and Alice held the bannister tightly as she paused on the second last step from the bottom. She straightened her back and steeled her resolve. She *would* find out how to get home.

In that moment, she decided she would risk telling Branton the truth. She trusted that he would not throw her out or abandon her wherever they were on the estate when she told him. She would get him to take her to the stones and she would show him. A slight smile curved her lips; perhaps he might think she was mad, but she would have to take that risk.

As she stepped down into the entry hall, Lord Branton came through the door on the side. He was wearing a riding cloak in a dark rich blue and the colour picked up the blue-black sheen of his hair.

Again, Alice smiled to herself. The more she smiled, the more her fear receded.

She would have to look on the bright side of things. She had been fortunate; she could have ended up in a manor held by a portly, red-faced drunken lord. Someone who resembled the portraits she had seen of Henry the Eighth.

Branton was very pleasant to the eye, and he was a kind and gentle man.

The smile was still on Alice's lips as he walked across to her. 'Who is the king? Or is it a queen?' she asked.

She should have paid more attention to her history lessons, but history from a book had held no interest for her at school.

Branton looked at her with that same strange expression that she had seen on his face a few times. 'Why, it is King Henry the Seventh, of course.'

'How long has he been king?' Alice asked as she followed Branton through to the back of the manor.

'Sine 1485 when he defeated Richard the Third on Bosworth field.'

'Who is his queen?'

Branton's voice was patient as he replied. 'King Henry is a clever man. He cemented his claim to the throne by marrying Edward the Fourth's daughter, Elizabeth of York.'

'Is he a good king?'

Branton took her arm as they stepped out onto the uneven cobblestones at the back of the manor. There had been no sign of anyone else, and again she was grateful for the gentleman that he was. 'You must have been out of the country for a long while if you do not know Henry is a good king.'

'Perhaps. I will tell you where I have been as we ride.'

'And yes, Alice, to answer your question, he is a very good king. He has been a very good monarch for the wool industry and the embargo on the Flemish wool in retaliation for the Netherlands' support of that scoundrel, Warbeck, has benefitted us greatly in the country.' He paused and stared out over the fields. 'Too much at times as it has caused local unrest. But enough of that. Come, we shall set out otherwise there will not be enough left of the day to show you the estate.' Pride filled his voice, and Alice decided she would not raise the issue of where she had come from or ask to go to the stones until he had had the opportunity to show her the land he was obviously proud of.

The big black horse was ready for them to mount and Alice nervously remembered how high it was once she was up there.

'Climb up onto that wooden stool,' he said.

A different sort of tension held her when Branton's hands went around her waist, and before she knew Alice had been effortlessly lifted from the stool and she was sitting on the horse; this time both her legs were on one side, and she felt as though she was going to fall off.

Before she could move, Branton had swung himself over the horse and was sitting behind her.

'Lean back into me and hold the pommel'—he gestured to the solid leather thing at the front of the saddle— 'and I assure you, you won't fall off.'

'I certainly hope not,' she said with a laugh. 'I've had enough adventure to do me a lifetime.'

Branton laughed with her, and then clicked his tongue, but before the horse could move forward, there was a clattering on the cobblestones behind them.

Branton swung the horse around and Alice felt the tension in his body as two horses cantered into the courtyard.

A small white horse carried a woman. She looked demure and her eyes were downcast as they both looked at her, but Alice had seen the expression that she had swiftly covered before she looked down. A large man with straw-coloured hair sat astride a reddish-brown horse.

Chestnut, Alice thought, putting her head down as that seemed to be the correct behaviour.

'Good morning to you both,' Branton said.

'Good morning, my lord.' The man's voice was deep.

'Good morning, Branton.' Although her voice was pleasant, the look the woman directed their way was certainly not. A shiver ran down Alice's back at the venom in the woman's eyes.

'We cannot tarry as the morning is getting late. I believe you are here to see Mistress Oatley, Isabelle.'

'I am, but I had hoped to take refreshment with you, and have a word to you first, Branton.'

Her lips drew into a pout when Branton replied.

'I do not have time today, perhaps you could come back next week. I am very busy with the sheep this week.'

'Oh?' The delicate blonde eyebrows arched and almost disappeared beneath the woman's headpiece, as she stared at Alice.

'Yes. I hope Mistress Oatley can assist with whatever it is you are seeking,' Branton said, 'Good day to you both.'

Alice was surprised when he turned the mount around and they crossed past the stables and through a gate onto a path that led up a hill. She was surprised that he had made no mention of her, or introduced her, but then perhaps social habits were different in 1496.

Chapter 14

The clouds had cleared, and warm sunshine poured down from a pale blue sky as Black carried them up the hill. Branton did not speak and gradually Alice relaxed as she became used to the movement of the horse beneath her. The air was fresh and clean, and the only sound was the creak of the leather saddle as they moved, and the occasional bird twittering when the horse moved past the thickets of small trees.

Alice also had become accustomed to—and was enjoying the feel of Branton's chest against her back. It was strange; she had had little experience with the opposite sex, but there was something about him that had instilled an innate trust in her. The silence was easy as the horse reached the top of the hill.

She drew in a deep breath as they reached the crest. Ahead of them lay a patchwork of fields laid out in long narrow rows. Each third field was fallow, and beyond the fields she could see the spires of a town.

Glastonbury.

Branton pulled on the reins and the horse came to a halt. Alice cried out as she tipped forward when Black put his head down to nibble at the lush green grass around them.

Branton's arms went around her and he chuckled. 'Don't worry, I won't let you fall. You are not used to being on a horse, are you?'

'No. Would you believe yesterday was the first time I have ever been on the back of a horse?'

She felt him nod behind her and she sensed the smile behind his words. 'I would.'

Alice gestured to the fields ahead; below the strips of cultivated land were green fields dotted with sheep. 'Is that all your land?'

'Yes, the estate is large. One of the largest in the shire. We grow hay and barley and rye, and the crops are looked after by Robert. I supervise the sheep. Mr Hodges grows the food we need at the manor, and we often have enough to share with our tenants. He has cabbages, onions, peas and beans growing this spring. Mrs Hodges insists on looking after the pigs and our geese.'

'Was Robert the visitor who rode in as we left?'

Before he answered, Branton swung his leg over and slid from the horse without warning her, and Alice grabbed at the pommel. She looked down at him as he held his arms wide. With a deep breath she leaned over, and he gripped her waist and lifted her down to the grass. She stood there as he lifted down a small bag that had been attached to the saddle.

'Yes, Robert is one of my tenant farmers and as well as looking after the estate crops he has a house and a small holding for himself.'

Alice nodded. 'And that was his wife with him?'

'No, Isabelle is his sister.'

'She is very beautiful.' Despite the nasty look that had been directed her way, Alice decided she could be gracious. She was also intrigued as to what the relationship was with Branton, but his answer was vague.

'Yes, she is a good woman,' was the brief reply. 'Come, Alice, it is your turn to tell me about your home.' Branton led the way to a large beech tree and took off his cloak, spreading it on the grass for her to sit.

Alice sat down as gracefully as she could. The cloth that her dress was made from was very stiff and the chemise had rubbed at her legs as the horse had moved beneath her.

Branton sat beside her and opened the leather bag. He pulled out two apples and a handful of dried figs, and a metal flask. 'Unfortunately, our cherry trees are only still in flower, and you cannot taste them as yet.' He lifted his head and looked at her intently.

Heat ran up Alice's neck as his gaze lingered. She was aware of his interest and her body responded with a warm quiver in her stomach. She dropped her gaze to look at the apple he had handed her. The skin was red and shiny, and it was one of the largest apples she had ever seen.

'Perhaps you can visit again when the cherries are ripe,' he said softly.

Alice looked up and Branton's eyes were still intent on her as he bit into the apple. A trickle of juice ran down to his chin and she smiled but resisted the urge to reach out and wipe it.

'If I can get back to my home, I doubt very much that I will be able to visit again.'

'Tell me why. Do you have a husband?'

She shook her head. 'No.'

'A father who will not let you travel?'

'No.'

'You live in a nunnery and you have run away?'

'No.' Alice sighed and bit into her apple to avoid conversation while she thought of what to say.

'You have intrigued me, Alice. I have never spoken to a woman like this before—please believe me—but I feel as though there is a strange connection between us. It is as though I have known you for a much longer time than one day. I had wool to take to Dunster today, but I ignored that so I could be with you. I think you have bewitched me.' His smile was wide.

Alice put the apple down on the cloak and folded her hands in her lap. 'There is no bewitching. I know what you are saying because I feel that connection too. As you say I have known you merely hours, but I know that I can trust you, and that it is safe to be with you.' She lifted her head and her voice shook with emotion. 'I even wonder if it is because of that connection that I have been brought to this . . .this place.' That thought had come to Alice as they rode up the hill. There had to be a reason behind her arrival in this time.

Perhaps the answer was Branton.

And perhaps she was being extremely foolish and that was merely wishful thinking to explain the inexplicable.

Branton moved closer and took her hand. 'Please tell me your story, Alice.'

Chapter 15
Branton

Branton looked down at the pale white hand resting in his. Alice's fingers were cold, and he put his other hand over hers to warm them.

'Please don't be afraid to tell me. I will not judge you.'

Her eyes were sad as she looked at him. 'I am not afraid of being judged. I am afraid you will think I am crazy.' She shook her head. 'But you probably have never heard that word, I would guess.'

'No, it is not familiar to me.'

'Deranged? Mad? Insane?'

He shook his head.

'I know! Village idiot?'

'No, Alice, it is as though you are speaking another language to me.' *As she had yesterday with her talk of unknown things,* he thought.

She closed her eyes and Branton let his eyes linger on her face. Her skin was fair, her eyes tipped up at the corners, but brushed beneath with faint purple shadows. Her nose was fine and straight, and her lips red and full. A long strand of dark hair had fallen from beneath her headpiece, and without thinking he lifted it up and twirled it around his finger.

Her eyes flew open and held his. 'I know! A lunatic. Do you know what a lunatic is?'

'I know the Latin word *lunaticus*. It describes a person whose actions have been touched by the moon.'

'Good, that is close enough to the meaning I am trying to get across to you. When I tell you my story, I don't want you to think that I also have been "touched by the moon".' She leaned forward and her breath, sweet from the apple, warmed his lips. 'I want you to believe me. You *must* believe me. And not to believe that I am trying to bewitch you.'

He let go of her hand as she moved away, her cheeks pink with colour.

'I promise I will listen to you,' he said.

'When I was a little girl, I hid in our cellar one day and I heard my mother talking about her fears. At the time it meant nothing to me. The story of two children going missing from the village near our cottage. We lived here near Glastonbury in our cottage, and I was so young, I don't even know what the village was called. I believe it was because of Mother's fear that we moved to London.' Alice's eyes welled with tears as she continued. 'We lived there as I grew up, and then the war came. My father and then my mother were killed in the war'—she lifted her hand as he raised his eyebrows— 'I will tell you about the war when I finish. I travelled back down to our cottage as I wanted to get away from London. I had no home there anymore. It was bomb—destroyed—in the war. I was only in the cottage for one night and I set out for the village to get some food, and that is when you found me.'

Her voice broke, but Branton did not touch her even though he wanted to. He would let her finish her story; he was fascinated by her words and her outline of events.

'I don't believe my cottage is there now. In fact, I know it's not. This is where you must believe me and try to help me get back to my home . . . back to my . . . back to my time.'

He was aware of his eyes widening as she spoke those last words. He reached out and took her hand in his as distress took hold of her.

'Branton, I am not from this time. . . your time. From the now. I know it sounds unbelievable, but I have come through the stones from a different time. I come from a time in the future. Many, many years in the future. We are in the middle of an horrendous war, and that war killed my parents, and set me on my path here. What I can't understand is *why* I am here. Here in this place, in this time.'

Branton looked at her for a long moment, gently cradling her hand in his, before he spoke. Her fingers were clenched within his, and her lips were set in a straight line as she stared back at him, uncertainty in her eyes.

'Do you think I am a lunatic?' she asked

He shook his head slowly. 'No, I don't believe you are. I believe you are genuinely lost. What you have told me is hard for me to understand, but it is not the first time I have heard of the magic of the stones.'

Her eyes widened and she smiled. 'You have heard of that happening before? Of someone arriving here?'

'I have heard stories, and there was an old woman in the village when I was a boy who would disappear for long periods and then reappear as though she had never been gone. I have also heard of others, more recently, who have come here and said they were from the future.'

Branton was not ready to tell Alice that there was a child close by who had said that in the past year.

She put her other hand to her chest and expelled a deep sigh. 'Oh, I was so worried that you would think I was lying . . . or mad.'

He smiled at her. 'No, I do not believe you are "mad". However, the problem is how can I help you return to your time?'

Alice pulled her hand from his and flung her arms around his neck. 'Oh, you really do believe me!'

Branton rested his head against hers.

They sat still and quiet for a moment before Alice lifted her head. 'Branton, can I ask you one thing?'

'You can.'

'Would you mind terribly if I took this contraption from my head? I can put up with the scratching clothes, but this *thing* is giving me a headache.'

With a laugh he reached over and unwound the band that was holding the headpiece in place. 'I think that is a fair exchange for you telling me a little of the future.'

Her eyes held his and Branton's hand stayed on her coiled hair as his gaze lowered from her eyes to her softly parted lips. Unable to explain or justify his action, he lowered his head and claimed her lips with his.

Chapter 16

Alice sat on the window seat in the room she had slept in. The room was becoming more familiar to her, and she was grateful that she had her own place, private and safe, where she could think.

And write down her experiences.

She gripped her lead pencil tightly as she wrote in her notebook. When she got home—and she *would* get home—she would read this and wonder if it had really happened.

It had seemed like a dream, but despite where she was, and her fears, it had been a wonderful day.

Not only did Branton believe me, he promised he would do everything in his power to help me go home. After he kissed me, we talked. I cannot find words to describe his kiss, so I will not try. There is no need as the memory will stay with me forever.

We sat on Branton's cloak as the westering sun lowered in the sky and painted the clouds in gold and purple. He asked me questions about the future, and I regretted so much not paying attention in my history lessons. About the only thing I could remember was that the next king, Henry the Eight had six wives and had executed two of them.

I said to him jokingly he should come back with me, it is all written in the history books. Branton sat up, interested, and I shook my head.

Books? he asked.

Yes, our history is written down and is accessible to everyone.

His look was incredulous. Even after five hundred years? he asked, and I told him of the ancient history we knew. The Greeks, the Romans, and the Egyptians.

I would love to come and see that, he said with his eyes wide. And what about farming and wool? Do you still have farms?

We do. I laughed but then I shook my head.

No, it is dangerous enough for me to try to go back.

I still don't know if I am brave enough to attempt it, but Branton has assured me that we will go to see Granny Irvine's daughter to see if she knows anything of the stones.

Branton kissed me again before we remounted Black, the horse, who I am becoming quite fond of.

Strangely since I have been here, my grief for Mother and Daddy has receded and the pain is now almost bearable.

Alice put the pencil down and put her notebook on the table next to the window. She stared out over the fields and realised for the first time that she could see the three stones from the window in her room. The sun was about to slip beneath the horizon, and she stared, certain she could see a blue glow emanating from them. She jumped to her feet and pressed her face to the pane of glass. As she watched, the sunlight crept further and further west along the forest until the sun was almost gone.

As the sunlight disappeared a bright blue flash came from the middle stone and lit up the air for a brief second.

Alice gasped and put a hand to her mouth. Perhaps the stones were aligned to the sun? She thought back to yesterday; her thoughts frantically churning. Yesterday when she had touched the stone and fallen through time, it had been almost noon when she had made her way to the village. Now the blue light had flashed again at sunset. She would rise early in the morning and would watch to see if the light flashed at sunrise.

So, if she was going to try to get home, should she go down and touch the stone at noon? Or at sunset?

How could she guarantee that she would get back to her time? Did the time of the day affect the time that she would go back to? Perhaps she should try noon.

##

Alice rose before dawn the next morning. She yawned as she stumbled out of the soft bed and pulled her cloak around her shoulders for warmth. The air was chilly, and she rubbed her hands on her bare arms beneath the cloak as she stood at the window. The dark stones were silhouetted against the dawn sky. As the sky lightened, she waited patiently.

Movement in the courtyard at the front of the manor caught her attention and she briefly took her eyes from the stones. As she watched a horse and rider cantered up the drive. A moment later, Branton appeared, mounted on Black, and he rode off into the dark with the visitor. Alice turned her attention back to the east and the stones. As the first light tinted the eastern sky a pale apricot, and then a rose gold shot with threads of silver, Alice waited, not taking her eyes away again. As the sun cleared the horizon, the stones flashed blue just as she had hoped.

She had been right. It was to do with sunrise, noon and sunset. Feeling very satisfied, she turned to make her way back to the warm bed, but another movement caught her attention. A figure had appeared beneath the middle stone, and she knew the person had not been there before. Slowly, the person made their way up the hill towards the village.

Alice narrowed her eyes. It was too distant to see who the person was, but she vowed that somehow, she would find out. She made her way back to the soft feather bed and crawled in between the still warm covers. Closing her eyes, she tried to think of a way home, but sleep soon claimed her.

Chapter 17
Branton

Branton rode alongside Robert as they made their way to the eastern side of the estate. The stones stood dark and cold in the predawn, and he gave them a passing glance wondering if Alice was right. She had told him her theory of the blue light as they had sat beneath the beech tree yesterday.

When they returned to the manor, she had retired to her room and had declined his invitation to dine with him. Disappointment had filled him, and he worried if he had been too forward when he had kissed her.

He had not been able to hold back, and Alice had returned his kisses willingly. On the ride back to the manor she had leaned back into his body, much more relaxed than when they had set out in the middle of the day. He could not get her out of his thoughts.

'My lord!' Robert's voice pulled him from his musing as the sun cleared the eastern horizon.

'What is it?' Branton pulled on Black's reins and kept his voice low.

'There is someone ahead. Near the stones.'

Dread pooled in Branton's gut and he leaned forward peering into the half-light, praying it wasn't Alice. They waited in the dark near a copse of trees and when the figure approached, Branton called out.

'Who goes there?'

Footsteps crunched in the leaves on the forest floor and then a woman's voice called out.

'It is only I.'

'And who is that?' Robert replied.

'Mistress Irvine.' As she spoke, the woman stepped into the copse where they waited.

'What are you doing on the estate at sunrise?' Branton demanded.

'I was picking mushrooms,' she replied.

Branton leaned forward in the saddle as she stood in the dark beneath a tree. 'They are in that sack you carry? I would have thought you would carry a basket for mushrooms, mistress.'

'No, I found none, so I am going back to the village.'

'What is in your sack?' The sack was misshapen from something bulky inside.

'A digging implement.'

For a moment Branton considered demanding that she showed him, and then on further thought, he realised there was no reason to. She was obviously not interfering with the sheep, although he did have his suspicions about what she was doing here.

'Very well. Have a good day, Mistress Irvine.'

Robert's voice was grim as she disappeared into the dark of the forest. 'What was that about? Do you think it is her husband who is interfering with the sheep? Do you think he may be the culprit? He's always been a surly man.'

'Perhaps,' Branton replied. 'Come and we will check on the flock in the eastern field.' He was thoughtful as they made their way across the estate. Mistress Irvine had appeared very suddenly as the sun had risen and she had appeared beside the stones. He suspected that she had more to hide than a few missing sheep.

##

The foray into the fields had been time wasted, as there was no sign of anyone interfering with the sheep, and on a head count the sheep were all accounted for.

Robert left Branton at the front entrance to the estate. 'You are going back to the manor?' he asked.

'Yes, there are things I have to attend to,' Branton replied.

Robert raised his eyebrows. 'Isabelle was very upset yesterday when you did not have time to speak with her.'

Branton held his gaze and drew himself straight in the saddle. 'Be careful, Robert with what you say.

You may be my friend, but you do not question what I do.'

Robert lifted one hand, and his voice was cold. 'I did not question you, my lord. I was merely passing comment on my sister's state of mind.' He turned the horse away and was soon out of sight.

Branton was cross that he had let Robert's words rankle. Was he risking a longstanding friendship, and the possibility of taking a suitable wife because of the presence of one woman who had been in his manor house for one day?

A fascinating woman who he could not get out of his thoughts. Impatiently, he clicked his tongue and Black turned towards the manor. Perhaps Alice was in the dining room, and he could break his fast with her.

Or should he ignore her presence and get on with the life he had had before she arrived?

Chapter 18

Alice had been sitting in the parlour when Branton came in from the stables. She had almost thrown her arms around him when he had suggested that they go to the town that morning. She had restrained herself as Mistress Oatley was in the parlour. Alice merely inclined her head with a quick glance at the housekeeper who had come in to take the tray and agreed that yes, she would like to see the town.

Dressed in the same borrowed clothes as yesterday Alice had managed to wind the headband around her hair so that it was not as tight but still held her braids in place. She had rinsed her own underwear in a little of the water from the jug in her room and had placed them on the windowsill to dry after Mistress Oatley had left the room last night. They had still been damp when she had slipped them on this morning but wearing damp underwear was better than the scratching of that rough wool against her nether regions.

Once again Alice was on the back of the horse with Branton as they set out from the stables towards the village.

'Where are we going? Who are we going to see?' She was much more talkative than she had been yesterday. A good night's sleep in that soft bed had made her feel much better, and she exclaimed and pointed to the flowers and the trees as they rode a different path than the day before. It was strange not having a clock to set the day by, and she guessed from the position of the sun it would be about ten o'clock.

She frowned. Not knowing the time would make it hard to know when it was exactly noon when she tried to go back through the stones.

And that was what she was going to try. Whether or not she would tell Branton, she wasn't sure of, as yet. As she was also unsure of why they were going to the town; she hoped it was to see the family of the old granny that he had talked about.

Life was so different here to what she was used to. Although it seemed much simpler, there was still work to be done to ensure that people were fed and had a productive life. And the characters that she had met were no different from people in 1941. Some friendly, some surly and some . . . well . . . plain rude. The woman called Isabelle came to mind.

The horse crested another hill as they headed towards the town and Alice looked down at Branton's arms, holding her even closer to him on this morning. Ahead of them were some small cottages with a couple of dogs lying on the grass, and some chickens picking at the grass on the side of the path.

'This is one of the villages on my estate,' Branton said. 'Some of the workers and their families live here.'

The path followed a brook that babbled over mossy stones and widened as they drew level with the cottages. A half dozen thatch roofed buildings surrounded a tiny green, and Alice noticed a water mill on the bank of the side stream.

'What does the mill do?'

'It is where the wheat is ground to produce the flour. And further upstream there is another village that services a mill where we use the stream for fulling.'

'Fulling?' Alice frowned. 'I do not know that word.'

'It is where the mill powers the water hammers to shrink and thicken cloth. Along with our sheep, it makes our estate a very productive enterprise.'

'It sounds very busy.'

'It is, and it keeps our workers content as well as busy. We are much better off here than many other estates where there is dissention.'

'I would think it was to do with having a just and generous lord.'

'I am fortunate. My father set a good example for me and it was easy to continue his work.'

'Who lives here?' Alice pointed to the cottages that they were passing.

'They are the cottages where the mill workers live. They are still tenants of Brue Manor, and belong to the estate. As do the people from all of the villages on the estate.'

They both looked ahead as a cry of distress came from the other side of the last cottage.

'I am not Amelia Davies!' A girl of about twelve years ran out across the path and headed for the bank of the stream.

'Amelia, don't be foolish. I did not mean it.' A boy of a similar age ran towards the path but stopped and stared when he saw his lord approaching on the huge horse. He put his head down and skulked back behind the cottage, but the young girl hadn't noticed their approach.

Her back was to them as she stood with her hands on her hips. 'Hugh Jenkins, you come back out here. We will sort this once and for all. I will not take the name of Davies. It is not my name.'

The girl turned and her mouth dropped open as she looked up at the big black horse. Colour ran up her face and she looked to the ground.

'Are you all right, miss?' Branton asked.

'Yes m'lord.' Her eyes stayed on the ground and then she lifted them when they went to ride past her. As she looked directly at Alice, the girl's eyes narrowed, and her mouth dropped open. She whispered something to herself and put one hand to her mouth before she took off at a run.

Alice stared after her; it was strange, but the girl had seemed familiar to her, but she didn't know why.

Branton hadn't appeared to notice anything untoward and he nudged the horse along the path.

Soon they had reached the outskirts of a small settlement.

'Is it a village or a town?' Alice asked as she looked ahead at people milling around.

'It is a town. The village we came through is one of five on my estate. This is the town where the monastery is, and it is more crowded today as it is market day. I brought you in as I know Mistress Irvine will be here at her stall. It is better than going to her cottage.'

Alice's eyes widened as they approached a square where there were what appeared to be dozens and dozens of tent-like stalls. Branton dismounted and held his arms open for Alice to slide down—she was getting quite skilled at this horse riding—and then he opened a gate and the horse went into a large open field where other horses grazed. Branton held his arm out and Alice slipped her hand through his elbow, feeling self-conscious as several stall holders seemed to be taking a great interest in them.

He led her past several stalls, and Alice took interest in the food and wares on sale. The market was busy, there were food stalls that gave out delicious aromas and smaller stalls with dozens of eggs, and chickens in wooden latticed boxes. A plethora of stalls covered all four sides of the square, sometimes three deep. Others walked by carrying their wares in baskets and called to the crowd milling between the stalls.

Her head moved from left to right as she took in the busy scene. At one stall she stood staring at a man working on a loom, Branton chuckled beside her.

'You are fascinated by this market. You should see the annual fair. It goes for two weeks, and there are so many different goods and wares on sale, people travel for miles to come to Glastonbury. Merchants come from Europe and display fine clothes, wines, spices and lace.'

'It is nothing like I imagined here,' Alice whispered, leaning into him. 'There is so much more. I don't mean the market, I mean your time.'

Branton leaned down and his forehead briefly touched hers. Warmth ran down Alice's back and her fingers tingled.

'I am pleased you are enjoying the spectacle, but we have to find Mistress Irvine. I am not sure where she sets up her stall. I don't usually come to town on market day,' he said.

'My lord!'

Alice pulled away from Branton as a shrill voice called out to him. Her stomach sank as she recognised the woman from the courtyard yesterday—the sister of the man who looked after the crops. A woman who was quite interested in the lord, she suspected.

An unexpected and unfamiliar shaft of jealousy settled in Alice's chest, and she frowned. She had no right to Lord Branton, despite his kiss yesterday, and no reason to feel possessive of him.

Branton leaned over and spoke quietly. 'You are a relative of my mother's travelling to London from Cornwall. Don't say anything.'

Alice nodded and focused her eyes on the stall to the left. Bright bolts of wool hung over a table and a crowd of women had gathered and were touching the woven fabric, talking quietly.

'My lord, it is most unusual to see you at the town market,' the woman said.

'Good morning to you, Isabelle.' Branton's hand rested on Alice's wrist and the warmth of his fingers reassured her. 'This is my mother's cousin, Mistress Alice from Bodmin. She is on her way to London.'

Alice went to nod a silent greeting, but the woman was not even looking at her.

'I wish to speak to you, Branton. I need your advice on a private matter. When will your cousin be gone?'

'I am not sure, Isabelle. I will probably wait a few weeks until the wool has been sent to the merchants, before I escort Alice to London.'

'Very well. I shall come tomorrow morn.'

'No, it will be a wasted time for you. I will not be there. The estate is taking many of my hours each day.'

Alice kept her features bland as Isabelle's eyebrows rose and she went to speak, but Branton cut her off.

'Come, Alice. We must be quick. Good day, Isabelle.'

The look of pure venom that was directed at Alice was not attractive. As they walked away, she lifted her eyes to Branton.

'Have I caused trouble for you?'

'No, you have not. Mistress Isabelle is too used to getting her own way. Ah, I see Mistress Irvine in her booth. Again, please don't speak, just listen to what is said.'

Alice nodded as they approached a stall holding a variety of bowls fashioned from wood and pewter.

The woman bobbed in a half curtsey as she greeted Branton. 'My lord,' she said as she directed a curious look at Alice.

'Mistress Irvine, I need to speak with you. Is there someone who could look after your stall for a time?' Branton picked up a pewter bowl that had a raised pattern around it. 'This is very fine work. I did not know we had craftsmen on the estate who do such fine work. Who created this?'

Alice was watching Mistress Irvine and noticed the colour that flamed up her neck. 'I get my pewter from elsewhere, my lord.'

'I suspected you might. Now may we have a private word?'

The woman summoned a boy who was sitting at the back of the tent.

'James, mind the stall for me.'

At the corner of the square where her stall was located, another road led down a hill. Alice was surprised to see some buildings that looked like shop fronts. It was more modern that she would have expected for this time.

'Are they—' She broke off as Branton squeezed her hand reminding her not to speak.

Halfway down the hill a flat seat was set into a stone wall and Branton gestured for Alice and the other woman to take a seat. He stood in front of them, his focus on Mistress Irvine.

Alice wondered what he wanted her to hear. She folded her hands demurely in front of her waist and waited.

Chapter 19
Branton

Having worked with many different tenants and serfs since his father had passed, one thing that Branton had learned was patience. He knew that Mistress Irvine had knowledge of the stones, and if it took until sundown for her to share her knowledge, so be it; he would wait.

'I don't have long, my lord. My boy is not good on the stall.' Mistress Irvine's eyes darted from right to left as though seeking escape.

Branton leaned back against the high wall and folded his arms. The street was empty; the townsfolk were all up in the square browsing the stalls.

'Mistress Irvine, I'd like you to tell me why you were out in the fields so early this morning.'

The woman lifted her chin. 'I have already told you, my lord, I was picking mushrooms.'

'That's very interesting,' he replied. 'I have roamed those fields since I was a boy, and I have no recall of any mushrooms on that part of the estate.'

'That's right, my lord. I told you I found none.'

'What was in the sack you were carrying, and where did you appear from so suddenly? There was no sign of you as we rode down the hill.' Branton stared at her and she looked away.

'I was there. I saw you coming.' Her lips were set in a mutinous line.

'Tell me if that is where your mother used to go.'

Her head flew up. 'Where are you talking about?'

'Wherever you were before we saw you. I know you are a traveller, Mary.' He kept his voice even and soft and was pleased to see her eyes widen as she put a hand to her head. He glanced at Alice. Her eyes were wide and fixed on Mistress Irvine.

Sympathy shot through him when he saw her expression.

Hopeful, scared, interested.

He would help Alice as best he could.

'I do not know what you speak of.'

As he watched Mistress Irvine's breathing quickened.

'Mary, please we need to know the truth. I will not interfere in your business. Wherever you get your pewter and wooden bowls from, it will remain a secret with me. I won't tell anyone—I mean Mistress Alice and I will not speak of what you say—but we must know about the stones. What your mother passed down to you. How you know to travel.'

'If I did know anything, why would you need to know, my lord?' Her voice was meek.

To Branton's shock, Alice dropped to her knees in front of Mistress Irvine. She grasped the woman's hands.

'*I* need to know. I need to go home. It *was* you I watched from the manor this morning. I saw the blue flash at sunrise as you came through the stones. Oh mistress, please tell me. I need to know how I can get home.'

Mistress Irvine stared at Alice, her eyes wary. 'Some said that my mother was a witch. How can I know that this is not a trap, to trick me into saying something that you want to hear? Something to be used against me?'

'Mary, how long have you known me?' Branton asked.

'Since your mother carried you in her belly.'

'Do you think I would do anything to harm you?'

She shook her head, before she turned to face Alice. 'How far have you come, mistress?' she asked.

Chapter 20

Alice sat straight and fought the emotion choking her as they rode back to the manor. Branton seemed distant and she held herself stiffly away from him as she clung to the pommel with both hands. Tears tightened her throat, but she would not give into them. Even though she had listened to what Mistress Irvine had said and believed it to be the truth it was hard to accept.

She had been right in her assumption about the stones being linked to the passage of the sun.

But it seemed she had missed the time to go back.

By one day.

Tears welled in her eyes and she lifted one hand and brushed them away impatiently.

'One month after the spring equinox, the sun moves and does not align with the stones,' Mistress Irvine said when she finally began to talk. Once she had begun to tell them what she knew, there had been no stopping her. She, and her mother before her, were frequent travellers; she did not say where—or when—

she travelled to, but it was simply to source goods to sell on her stall, and no further.

'Not everyone can travel,' she said. 'And in the same way, people who are born as travellers stumble upon the stones and travel without intent. My mother's mother taught her, as she taught me, and her mother before that. The knowledge has always been in our family.'

Alice nodded. *And in mine,* she thought.

Mistress Irvine's eyes held sympathy. 'That is what happened to you, mistress?' she asked.

Alice nodded again. 'Yes, it was without intent. I knew nothing of the stones, but I believe my mother did. All I want to know is how I can go home.'

Branton leaned forward. 'If the stones have closed as you say, when do they open?'

'One moon before the autumn equinox when the sun reaches the right place in the sky again.'

Alice stared at her. 'That would be in four months.'

'Months? I do not understand that, but it will be after four full moons at the end of the summer. Just after the harvest.'

Alice continued to hold the older woman's hands as she spoke. Her skin was rough, and her fingernails stained with dirt. 'Please tell me if I *will* be able to go back where I came from. How can I be sure?'

'My mother went to many places, and she taught me how to come back to where the time is right.'

'How?' Alice pleaded.

'You must go at the same time you came through, and you must touch the same stone in the same place as when you travelled here. What time of day did you come, young one?' she asked gently.

'In the middle of the day. At noon.'

'So that is when you will return, when the harvest comes around. Now I must get back to the market. My son is a lazy boy and will not call buyers to the stall.' She stood and before she walked away, she touched Alice's hand. 'If you need to talk to me again, my lord will show you which is my cottage.'

'Thank you,' Alice whispered.

As they approached the manor house, Branton turned the horse towards the hill. Alice was lost in her thoughts and barely noticed where they were going until Black stopped, and Branton was off and lifting her down.

As he had yesterday, he spread his cloak on the grass. It was a beautiful spring day—the sky was clear, the air was pure, and the woods were filled with the sweet sound of birdsong.

But Alice paid no regard to the pleasant afternoon as she sank to the ground, put her face into her hands and gave in to her distress.

Gentle hands held her and guided her to a comforting shoulder. As she cried Branton held her close, his hands rubbing her back in soothing movements.

'Hush, my sweet. It is not forever. Four moons is not a long time.'

Gradually Alice's sobs subsided, and she lifted her face to him, rubbing at her eyes with her knuckles. Her headpiece had come askew and she pulled it off angrily and placed it on the cloak. Her hair tumbled down over her shoulders; she had not braided it before they left today but had merely held it up under the headpiece with the band.

Branton's hands moved from her back as he lifted her hair and held her shoulders gently. Alice swallowed and stared up into his blue eyes. Each of his dark eyelashes was clearly defined and he stared back at her steadily. Her heart slowed down and dropped to a steady beat and her lips parted.

'Forgive me, but I must.' Branton leaned forward and his warm breath brushed her face like the touch of a butterfly wing. Her hair fell forward, and he lowered his head a touch closer. 'You have bewitched me, Alice. I should be taking care of you, but all I want to do is hold you and kiss you. Can you explain to me why I feel this way?'

She shook her head. 'I can't.'

'Do you know what I am feeling? Do you share this connection that I feel? I know it is such a short time, but I feel as though I know you so well. I have not felt like this before and as much as I know you are upset by Mistress Irvine's words'—his voice was rough— 'I am pleased that I will have you here with me for a while longer.'

Alice lifted one hand and cupped his cheek. Feeling confident enough to reach up and touch Branton was a new experience for her, but it felt right. She had no hesitation and had no fear of him.

With a groan he turned his face into her hand and kissed her open palm. Exquisite quivers danced in Alice's lower belly and she let out a soft sigh.

'You make me feel wanton,' she whispered. 'Do you know what that word means?'

Chapter 21
Alice - One week later

A week passed and Alice spent her days going out into the fields with Branton. The promised visit from Isabelle had not ensued, and Alice settled into the life of the manor. She became more settled and content as each day passed.

On her seventh night, she dined with Branton by flickering candlelight in the richly panelled dining room. Although it was spring, a low fire burned in the grate. Mistress Oatley had been to the market that day, and a feast had been laid out for them. She had also laid out a dress for Alice to change into, and there had been more clothes placed on the small table in her room as each day had passed. It appeared the housekeeper knew she would be staying at the manor and had grown more pleasant towards Alice as each day had passed.

The dress she wore tonight was sewn from velvet, a rich ruby red, and Alice had gasped when she had put it on and smoothed her hands over the beautiful fabric. The neckline was wide and scooped and showed an expanse of her fair skin. Puffed sleeves continued down to long sleeves that tapered to a point above her wrists. A black intricate choker had been laid out with the dress.

It was the most beautiful dress Alice had ever seen, and she had never worn anything of such a brilliant colour. She had pulled her fingers through her hair over and over until the tangles were gone, and then had styled it so a curled tress hung on one shoulder.

Branton's look of approval when she walked into the panelled dining room had sent longing spiralling through her. Their conversation was quiet as they dined, but she was aware of his eyes on her constantly.

As Mistress Oatley cleared away after they had eaten, Branton put up his hand.

'Please tell Mrs Hodges that was an excellent meal. You may both retire for the evening.'

The housekeeper nodded and took the tray, flicking a curious look at Alice, who was sitting at the table by Branton's side, rather than opposite him. He had moved the chair before Alice had sat at the large table so she was closer to him. Branton waited until Mistress Oatley had left the room, and then he reached over and took Alice's hand.

'Are you feeling better now that a week has passed? You have a healthy glow in your cheeks, and you don't look as sad this evening.'

When Branton had been out in the fields during the days, Alice had explored the house and gardens. She had learned much about the manor and had been surprised by how civilised life was in this time.

Wandering around the manor Alice had learned how a large manor house was run in the fifteenth century. It ran efficiently with few staff, and she began to feel welcome once Mistress Hodges and Mistress Oatley became used to her coming and going in the day. She spent time in the kitchen and the scullery with the cook. Mistress Hodges was a cheery plump woman and she had even shown Alice how to make pastry for the pigeon pie she baked one afternoon. Mistress Oatley had allowed her to help clean some wool carpet squares in the garden on a sunny morning, and they had laughed together when Alice's head piece had tumbled off as she had put all of her energy into beating the wool squares with the rounded piece of wood.

Mr Hodges had shown her around the grounds and told her the names of some of the unusual flowers she had not seen before. The intricate layout of the brick gardens in a herringbone pattern surprised her. It was as detailed and neat as some of the Royal gardens she had visited with her mother, albeit on a smaller scale. She had also discovered a small chapel behind the gardens where the deep stream ran along the fields to the water mill near the village.

Alice had spent a lot of time in the Great Hall decorated with huge tapestries and ornate lamps on the walls. All the rooms in the manor house were panelled with dark timber, and the walls in the Great Hall had intricate carvings around the mantlepiece.

The only room that she hadn't entered was Branton's suite at the end of the long hallway on the upper storey.

'Alice? You are lost in your thoughts.' Branton's deep voice pulled her from her musing.

'I'm sorry. What did you say?' His eyes were holding hers and Alice blushed as that pleasant quiver that had thrilled her over the past week, ran through her belly.

'Are you feeling better now that a week has passed?'

'I do. I have had time to think and I have accepted that I must wait until the autumn and I will look on my time here as a visit. A visit where I can learn about the past.' She didn't dare tell him that the main reason she was feeling so content was because of the kisses they had shared up in the woods for much of the afternoon.

As they had during each afternoon in the past week. Riding back to the manor on Black, with

Branton's arms around her had been like walking in the clouds.

At times, Branton's hand had brushed her breast through the linen dress, beginning that exquisite quiver. For a fleeting moment, Alice had wished that Mother was here so she could tell her how she felt, and then smiled, thinking it was not the sort of information that you would share with your mother.

'I will teach you whatever you would like to learn, dear heart.' His voice was rich and deep, and she looked down at the long elegant fingers holding hers.

***

Branton let his gaze linger on Alice. Two patches of pink sat high on her cheekbones, and she was all beauty as she sat straight looking at him with a softness in her gaze. Her hair glistened in the soft candlelight and her lips were parted; they were as red as the velvet dress that showed off an expanse of beautiful smooth skin. He stood and his legs trembled before he kneeled beside her chair.

'My dear Alice, I am in a quandary, and I cannot help myself speaking of what I feel. I know it is not right to say this. If you were my wife, I would not hesitate, but I cannot ask you to marry me because I know you will leave me after the harvest, and I don't know if I can stand that when the time comes. I would like to take you to my bed, but I know it would not be right.'

He closed his eyes as her hand moved to the top of his head and she caressed his hair. When he was away from Alice, he tried to rationalise this feeling that she caused to rise within him. It was like nothing he had ever felt before. When he was with her, he wanted to hold her and cherish her and protect her. Already the thought of her leaving him in the late summer was unbearable. Perhaps he could convince her to stay.

He must.

When he was away from her, the feeling lessened, but Alice stayed in his thoughts wherever he was. He was lovesick.

'Since I was nineteen years of age, I have thought myself in love on several occasions, but each time I hesitated when I thought of taking a wife.' He reached up and cupped her cheek as she looked down at him. 'I now know why. I have never felt a love like this.' He touched his heart with his other hand. 'It comes pure and untainted from my heart and soul. My heart that is yours alone.'

Tears hovered on Alice's lashes. 'I have never heard such beautiful words. I have never been loved by a man like that.' She lowered her head and spoke softly, and the colour in her cheeks deepened. 'I have never been loved by a man in any way.'

'Would you be my wife, sweet Alice?'

She shook her head. 'That would not be fair to you, as I must leave you, Branton.'

'Why must you?' The cry came from his heart. 'You told me yourself you have no one left to return to. Perhaps there is a force that brought us together for that very reason. You asked why you have come to my time. Perhaps love transcends time.'

Alice reached over and opened her arms, and Branton placed his head on her breast. There was no sound apart from the low wind that whistled through the window and made the candle sputter.

After a few moments, Alice stood and held out her hand. 'Take me to your bed, please, Branton.'

##

The act of being together brought an ecstasy to Branton such as he had never experienced. Afterwards he could not take his eyes off Alice as they sat naked on cushions in front of the fire in his bedchamber. Her pale skin glowed translucent in the firelight and a satisfied smile curved her lips.

'I did not hurt you?' he whispered as he passed her the tankard of wine that they were sharing.

'Oh no, you took me to a place that I had not even dreamed of. A place that I did not know existed.'

'A place that you would like to stay, perhaps? Marry me, Alice.' She passed him the tankard and he took a sip and regarded her steadily. 'Marry me, dear heart.'

'Give me time, Branton. This is all so new to me. But each day the feeling that I belong here with you grows stronger. But still I am frightened.'

'I will look after you. I would lay my life down for you.'

Chapter 22

Two months later, and after many wonderful nights spent in Branton's bedchamber, Alice had settled into life at Brue Manor. She had become used to the linen clothes and the different diet, but not so used to the outside privy, she thought with a smile.

Yet what she had still not adjusted to was the knowledge that her body's needs could be so quickly and wonderfully satisfied by Branton, and that she had no control over her desire. The desire that consumed them both each night and found completion in Branton's bedchamber.

On this morning, Alice set out for the market, after Branton had extracted a promise from her that she would go nowhere near the stones, no matter how curious she was. He was going away for two nights with Robert to see the wool merchant in Dunster.

'I promise,' she'd said as he held her close before they went down to dine together before Branton left. 'Besides, I am looking forward to wandering around the market.'

Alice had moved into his bedchamber and after Branton left she went up the stairs and pulled out her notebook. Her lead pencil had worn so short that she would not have it for much longer, and she was determined to find a writing implement at the market. Branton had given her four groats which she carried in a drawstring pouch at her waist.

She had almost filled her notebook with her observations, and feelings since she had arrived.

I am looking forward to attending the market and blending in with the crowds. In my months here, I have learned new words and paid attention to the way that the women speak, and I think I have been able to replicate it enough so that my language does not sound too different.

Life at the manor is good and becoming easier each day. Both Mistress Hodges and Mistress Oatley have been very kind to me. I think it is mainly because they see how happy Branton is these days. Mistress Hodges told me that it was wonderful to hear him laugh so much, as he had laughed before his father died.

Alice put the notebook on the window seat with the tiny stub of pencil that was left and reached for the light cloak that Mistress Oatley had brought her from the market last week.

As she left the house, she realised that she was truly happy. Taking a deep breath, she inhaled the fresh air redolent with the fragrance of flowers from the garden that was now a riot of colour. The weather had warmed, and summer and the harvest were not far off. Two full moons had passed, and she had one month to decide what she would do.

What was here for her?

Lord Branton of Brue Manor.

Alice pushed the thoughts from her mind; the prospect of visiting the market was too good to let worries crowd her mind. Not that it was a true worry; Alice was beginning to think that she would most probably stay and make a life here. What was there to go back to? A cold and empty cottage and the danger of war. A lonely life, with no family.

She was also holding a secret that would make her choice very simple.

As Alice approached the village near the watermill, children's voices drifted across from the banks of the stream. As she got closer two boys burst from the low undergrowth almost knocking her from her feet.

'Sorry, mistress,' they yelled, but their laughter did not hold any apology.

Alice shook her head and continued on, but soon became aware of footsteps behind her. A prickle ran up her neck, and she recalled Branton's warning to stay on the public path.

Well, she had done as he had asked, so there was no danger here. Or there should not be. She was close enough to the village to call for help if need be. Her fingers closed over the small drawstring bag which held the groats beneath her cloak.

Alice quickened her pace, but the footsteps got closer. She swallowed. and found the courage to turn around. Relief filled her and she stopped to let her heartbeat return to normal.

Putting a hand to her chest, she waited for the young girl to reach her.

'Hello. You are from the village, are you not?' Alice concentrated on broadening her vowels like Mrs Hodges did. The young girl stood beside her but did not speak. Her gaze was intent on Alice, and Alice stared back, that same familiarity tugging at her, and she was sure it wasn't because she had seen her in the village when she had first arrived.

'I've seen you a couple of times in the village, haven't I?' she said when the child didn't answer.

Finally, the girl nodded. 'Yes. My name is Amelia.' Again, she stared at Alice, seeming to wait for a reaction.

'Amelia?' she said slowly as a distant memory tugged. 'Amelia who?'

'They call me Davies here.'

'Ah, you are Robert's daughter.'

'No.' The cry was harsh. 'I am not. I said they call me Davies *here.*'

'What do you mean *here*?' Alice's fingertips tingled.

'Alice, don't you remember me?' The girl's lip began to quiver. 'Please say you remember me.'

'Why would I remember you?'

'We went to the village school and played hopscotch. When we were both little girls.' Her lip quivered. 'But now you are grown up and I'm not. But I was sure it was you, Alice. And now that you are close to me, I *know* it is you. Please help me.'

Alice's mouth dropped open. 'Amelia?' she finally managed to whisper. 'Amelia Adnum?'

The girl burst into tears and flung her arms around Alice's waist.

Alice held herself rigid as she smoothed her hand over Amelia's hair trying to soothe her. 'Hush, it is all right. I'm here. Calm down and we will talk.'

The deep gulping sobs quietened after a couple of minutes.

'Come and sit with me by the stream,' Alice said. Her thoughts were in a whirl. How could this girl be Amelia? But Alice knew she was; she could remember her from the village school in Pilton before they had moved to London. And Mr Jenkins had said she had been one of the children who had gone missing.

Alice shook her head as she led Amelia to the grassy bank, trying to clear her thoughts and make sense of what she was seeing.

"How old are you, Amelia?'

'I am twelve years old.' She gripped Alice's hand as though she would never let go. 'I came here when I was eight. I have been here for four years and I want to go home.' She began to cry again. 'I want my family. I want to go home to my house.'

Alice put her arms around her and let the child cry as she tried to make sense of what she was seeing and hearing.

Amelia had come through the stones when she was eight years old, at the same time that Alice had been eight years old. And now Amelia said she was twelve.

So, in those four years that Amelia had been here, Alice had aged eleven years. A cold prickle of fear ran down her back. Did that mean time passed differently?

What would that mean for her when—if—she went back through the stones?

##

It was a long time before Amelia was calm enough to talk and tell Alice what had happened.

'I was being naughty. My mum told me to come straight home from school. I wasn't allowed to go near the stones; she was right adamant about that.' She picked up a small rock and threw it into the water and it landed with a loud plop. 'I was curious, so I walked past the stones on my way to school one afternoon in winter. It was almost as though they called to me when I got near. I could hear singing.'

'What did you do?'

'I walked over and there was a little bit of stone sticking out low on the middle one. I reached out and touched it, and the singing got louder.' Her eyes were wide when she turned to Alice. 'And then I felt really sick. I fell down and I hit my head on the stone, and when I woke up,'—she hitched a sob and Alice reached out and took her hand again—'and when I woke up Johnny Jenkins and Hugh Davies were looking at me. They helped me up and took me to Hugh's father and told him they found me under the stones.'

'Is Hugh's dad Robert?'

Amelia nodded. 'Yes. He is a good man.'

'He seems to be. What happened then?'

'I tried to tell them what had happened when I touched the stone, but I wasn't allowed to talk about it. They said I had run away from my home, but I hadn't and now you're here, someone knows that I am telling the truth.'

'Have they treated you well?' Alice asked.

'They have. I help Elizabeth with the little ones, but it's not where I want to be. Do you know how we can get home, Alice? Please help me get home.' Her eyes were huge in her pale face, and Alice's heart broke for the child.

'I will do my best, Amelia. But we will have to wait until after the next moon. After the harvest.'

Chapter 23

Branton

Branton pushed Black hard on the last leg of the ride from Dunster as he was keen to get home to Alice. The meeting with the Flemish merchants in Dunster had taken an extra day—he had been away for three days, not two. King Henry had quarrelled with Philip of Burgundy, an import duty had been placed on English cloth and the negotiation on the price with the merchants had been protracted. In the end Branton agreed to their terms, simply because he was anxious about leaving Alice for that length of time.

He bid Robert farewell at the base of the hill near the village and spurred Black for the last mile of the journey home. It was a warm day and the horse was a lather of sweat by the time they rode into the cobblestoned courtyard.

Branton was pleased to see Mr Hodges and Peterkin, the stable boy, in the vegetable garden.

'Peterkin, see to my horse,' Branton said.

The boy took the reins, and Branton hurried across to the manor pausing only to sluice his face and neck in the pan of water outside the privy.

All was quiet in the house and he took the stairs two at a time to the first floor.

'Alice,' he called.

But she was not upstairs, neither in his suite or the guestroom. Worry began to coil in his stomach as he went down the stairs.

Mistress Oatley was dusting in the Great Hall when he went there after looking in the parlour.

'Mistress Alice is not here, my lord.'

The worry solidified into a hard ball. 'Not here? Where is she? There is no market today. I have just ridden though Glastonbury.'

Mistress Oatley pursed her lips. 'She has spent most of the past three days in the mill village. I tried to tell her it was not right, but she would not take heed of what I said.'

'Why? Why is she in the village, I mean?' Branton asked with a frown.

'I do not know but that is where I am sure you will find her.'

It didn't take long to saddle Bonnie, and Branton was on his way down to the mill village. Robert was still on horseback talking to one of the mill workers.

'Robert,' he called. 'Have you seen Alice?'

'No. What is wrong?'

Branton shook his head and rode on. He had never shared Alice's story with Robert. As much as he trusted his friend, it was not his story to tell.

He also didn't want to risk Robert telling either his wife, or Isabelle, that Alice was a traveller.

Turning the small horse, he rode towards the stones. He knew that Alice was fascinated with them and although she had promised that she would stay away, he still wanted to reassure himself.

He cantered down the hill, but the field was empty, and the stones stood silent in the late afternoon sunlight. A flash of colour ahead caught his attention, and as he stared at the stones, Branton's worry increased.

Chapter 24

Alice turned as she heard Branton call. She and Amelia had been walking in the woods picking wildflowers. They had spent the last three days together and Alice knew her presence had given Amelia hope of getting back to her family. The child had been happier each day and had been reluctant to leave Alice as the afternoon drew to a close.

'Wait here, Amelia.' She passed over the flowers that she was holding and ran up the hill. By the time she reached Branton, he had dismounted, and he held her close after she ran into his arms.

He kissed her and rested his cheek against hers. 'I was worried when you weren't at the house, but by the gods, it is wonderful to see you again.'

'It is wonderful to have you home. I missed you too. Very much,' she said quietly. As she had spent time with Amelia, Alice knew she had to tell Branton what she suspected.

'I don't think Bonnie will hold us both. You ride her and I will lead you home.'

'Wait one moment. I will just send Amelia home.'

'Amelia?'

Alice was surprised when Branton straightened and looked down the hill where Amelia stood with an armful of wildflowers. His mouth was set, and a frown creased his brow as he stared at the young girl.

'Why are you with a child from the village?'

The tone of his voice made her cross. 'Why shouldn't I be?'

He dropped his arms and Alice stepped back.

'Go and say your farewell. I will wait here. We shall talk later.'

##

Branton was distant as they dined, and his forehead seemed to be set in a constant frown. Finally, Alice could not stand it any longer, and she reached over and touched his hand.

'Did your wool sales not go well? Or have you had more sheep go missing?' Her voice caught as worry plagued her.

Or have you tired of me, was the awful thought flitting though her mind. Perhaps when he was away from her, Branton had realised that he no longer wanted her. Perhaps that would be the best outcome.

His eyes were tired as they finally met her gaze.

'I am sorry, dear heart. I have been preoccupied. Yes, to both of those questions.'

But what about the third that she was not brave enough to ask.

Do you no longer want me?

Her distress must have been evident because Branton reached over and squeezed her hand.

'I missed you while I was gone. It was as though I had left a part of me behind.'

'I missed you very much too.'

Branton pushed his chair back and pulled Alice up to her feet. 'Come and tell me what you have done while I was gone. Tell me what you bought at the market.'

She smiled as he pulled her onto his lap, and his arms held her close.

'I didn't get to the market. I met Amelia on the way.' Alice frowned, she didn't miss the tension in Branton's hold as she spoke of Amelia.

'Mistress Oatley told me you had been spending time in the village.'

'I need to speak with you, Branton. I have two very important things to talk to you about.'

His voice was sad. 'You have come to a decision as to what you will do after the harvest?'

'Let's go upstairs and talk in private.' Alice couldn't bear the unhappiness on his face. 'Don't worry, my darling. I do not want to leave you.'

'You do not *want* to? But you will?'

Alice stood and tugged at his hand. 'Take me to *our* bedchamber. This is my home.'

But Alice worried that the joy in his expression would not last when she told him her plan.

Chapter 25

Branton

'A child?'

'Yes, a child.'

Branton stared at Alice as disbelief took hold of him.

'The knowledge has made my decision to help Amelia easier.'

Branton shook his head. 'You have me confused. What do you mean help Amelia?'

Alice sat back and leaned against the bed.

'Branton, I know what it is like to be lost in a different time. I was very fortunate that it was you I encountered.'

'It was more than good fortune,' he said quietly as the joy from what she had just told him was dampened by her words. 'It was why you travelled to this time. It was for us. It was meant to be.' He knew Alice well enough to know what she was about to say, and he knew it was going to break his heart.

Especially now.

'I know that, and I believe it was as you say. Until I met Amelia, I knew what my decision would be. I had nothing to go back to, and every reason to stay here. Branton, you must know how much I love you.'

Branton shook his head and reached over and laid his hand on her stomach. 'You have more reason to stay here now. You have our child to think of. I cannot allow you to leave when you carry our child.'

When Alice had told him that she was sure she was carrying a child, joy such as he had never known had surged through him.

Alice reached out and put her hand on top of his. 'Yes, I carry our child and I will return to you. All I can think of, all I have been able to think of since I met Amelia and she told me of her plight, was what if it had been our child. I know how confused and scared I was when I came through the stones. Imagine what it would have been like for a small child of eight-years-old? Imagine if it had been our child? Would you not want someone to help them come back to us, if it happened to one of ours?'

'Alice, it is too dangerous.'

'I have been to see Mary Irvine and she has told me what I must do to take Amelia home safely, and then return to you. Branton?' Her voice broke and she reached out and put her hands on each side of his face as she spoke. 'I must do this, and I promise I will return to you.'

'I will come with you.'

Despair gripped him when Alice shook her head. 'No. I will take Amelia home and I will return immediately. I knew you would request that, and I asked Mary about it. She thinks it is—' Alice broke off.

'She thinks it is what, Alice?' He held her hands tightly as he waited, and she looked away from him for a second and then she took a deep breath.

She thinks it is enough of a risk that two of us will travel together.'

Branton held her gaze. 'Alice, I beg of you, please do not go. Set Amelia on her way and stay with me.'

Her voice was sad. 'I will not think less of you for those words, Branton, as I know the pain you feel. But I promise you this. I promise that I will come back to you.' She leaned forward and put her lips to his. 'For you. And for our child.'

***

Alice

Four weeks passed, and soon Alice and Amelia would travel home. The harvest had begun, and Alice and the young girl spent much time in the fields watching the workers. The weather had stayed clear, and the harvest began on the last quarter of the moon.

By Alice's calculations it was the second of August and the moon would be full in three weeks, just after the harvest festival.

Her nerves were beginning to fray. Branton had kept her close when he had been unable to change her mind, as though spending every minute with her helped make her leaving bearable for him.

As she sat with Amelia, Alice sighed. If it hadn't been for the excited anticipation of the young girl, she knew she would have changed her mind.

A week ago, there had been a lunar eclipse and Branton had been distraught, claiming it was a portent of doom for the journey that was getting closer each day.

'God has sent the eclipse to warn us, Alice. We have had this happen before, and there has always been a death soon after.'

Alice explained to him what an eclipse was, and despite his fear, Branton had been interested in the science of the explanation that she gave to him.

'If only I could come with you. There is so much I could learn.' He had finally accepted that he could not sway her determination to take this journey with Amelia.

Alice put one hand up to shade her eyes. Branton was in the middle of the field of rye. As she had taught him much of the scientific knowledge that she knew, he had taught her of what he knew best: the harvest.

'It is the culmination of our year's work, and that is why we will celebrate with a festival,' he explained as they had walked down together for the first day of the harvest.

'The timing depends upon the weather,' he explained. 'These last weeks of warm sun and gentle rain have ensured a good crop and the last three days of sunshine with no rain have created the perfect conditions for the harvest.' Branton's smile, which she had not seen as often in recent weeks, cheered Alice.

Workers had come from all of the villages to help bring in the crops. The wheat and rye were harvested first, followed by the spring grains, barley and oats, and most of Branton's attention had been on the harvest.

'How many more days now, Alice?' Amelia was lying on her back in the grass, with her eyes closed.

'One day less than what I told you yesterday, young lady.'

'So, twenty days plus one month?' Amelia sat up and looked over the field. 'You don't want to go anymore, do you, Alice?'

Alice put her hand to her stomach as a tiny flutter reminded her of the child she was carrying.

'I gave you my word that I will take you home, and I will do that.'

'But you will come back here, won't you?' Amelia said.

'I will.' Alice nodded, hoping with every ounce of her determination that she would be able to.

##

A week later, Alice was walking down to the oat fields to take Branton some bread and cheese for his noon meal. The harvest was in full swing, and he had told her that she had brought him luck. It was the best yield for over ten years. Amelia was helping Elizabeth with the children, and Alice knew that she would find it hard when the girl was gone.

As she reached the bottom of the hill, a bluish haze ahead turned her blood to ice. As she watched a shaft of light arced from the middle stone into the sky.

'No,' she whispered. 'It's too early. It was not what Mary Irvine had said would happen.' She paused and looked at the stones, but the light had gone, and for a moment she hoped it had been her imagination. Or was Mary wrong?

As she turned her eyes to the field on the right, Branton waved to her and pointed to the top of the field. Alice waved back and changed direction as she set off again. Her steps were slow as she worried about the light she had seen at the stones.

The hair on the back of Alice's neck rose as the world went quiet and still. The birdsong that had filled the air stopped as though a switch had been turned, and as the world around her began to go dark, the happy chatter from the harvesters that had carried across the fields to her, ceased.

Chapter 26
Branton

Branton flung the scythe to the ground and ran across the field as the sky darkened. The further he ran towards where he could just see Alice standing in the dim light the darker it became. Eventually he had to slow his steps and then stop as the world went completely dark. He looked up in the pitch dark to where the sun had been, and a measure of relief filled him as he saw the faint outline around the now dark sun.

Thank the Lord. It was another eclipse. Although he knew the scientific explanation for what was happening—thanks to Alice's instruction— his long-held superstitions came to the fore.

It was a warning for Alice not to travel. He knew it was not time yet, but Branton had seen the light come from the stones just before the world had gone dark.

'Alice,' he called. 'I'm coming. Where are you?'

'I'm over here.'

Branton followed the sound of her voice, and by the time he reached her, the sky had begun to lighten.

He wrapped his arms around her and before he could speak, she put her fingers to his lips.

'Don't say a word about omens or portents. It is simply a solar eclipse.'

'I know what it is.' He shook his head. 'And it is an omen. What you have to understand about our time is that things like sunrise and sunset, the moon, and the change of seasons, give order to our world, and our survival depends on it.'

'That may be so, but it does not mean that something bad is going to happen.' Alice lifted her lips for his kiss.

'I will hope and pray that you are right. I have little time to convince you to stay.'

'It will be good, my love,' she said. 'I promise you whatever it takes I will find you. Time has no meaning, and I will seize every opportunity I can to be with you.'

The sun came out in its full glory as the last of the moon passed over it, and the birds began to sing again.

'I promise you that when I am back, one day I will take you to my time, but only on the condition that this is where we will return to. I have found my home, and it is here with you, in your time.'

Branton couldn't help the smile that lifted his lips and he kissed her again. 'I told you months ago that you have bewitched me. I am very pleased that you have found your home. But you must promise me that you will find your way back to me.'

'I will, Branton. Whatever it takes, I will come home to you. I promise you that.'

Chapter 27

The solar eclipse of the eighth of August 1496 had left Alice unsettled. She hid her nervousness from Branton as best she could and kept her mood happy as the day that she and Amelia were to travel came closer. She was pleased that the harvest festival began five days before they were due to leave. The fourth day of the harvest celebration had been a magical day, and once Branton had escorted Alice home, he had gone back to celebrate with the harvest workers before they went back to their villages.

'I don't want to leave you even for an hour,' he said as he prepared to walk back down to the village square.

'I will be here when you return,' she said.

'I will try not to be late, but it could be well after dark. The workers have done an excellent job and I must show my appreciation.'

When Branton left, Alice turned to her notebook. The stub of her lead pencil was barely big enough to hold now, and she vowed that she would bring back a set of pencils when she returned.

The moonlight was shining on the marker stones window and a shiver ran down Alice's back. She rose and closed the heavy drapes, so she didn't have to look at them; she was dreading the journey with Amelia. She moved the candle closer to the side of the bed and began to write.

September 23rd, 1496

The last of summer has passed, and I can't believe that I am still here. I arrived in the spring and I must leave in the autumn before the cold and the shorter days set in.

Keats Ode to Autumn *is going around and around in my thoughts. I laughed. How wonderful would it be to visit the Lakes in the time of the Romantic poets?*

This afternoon we lay under the spreading beech tree down the hill from the watermill, I lay there with my head in Branton's lap reciting my favourite poem.

'While barred clouds bloom the soft-dying day,

And touch the stubble-plains with rosy hue;

Then in a wailful choir the small gnats mourn.'

'That's beautiful,' he said, repeating it as his fingers played with my hair. Every so often he would lean forward and brush his lips across my cheek. A delicious shiver would run down my back as his blue eyes with the long fringing black lashes held mine, sharing secrets that no one else could know.

If I record my days here, I will have those memories to revisit. But memories are cold comfort when you are alone. I will return. I must have faith.

The harvest festival is finished; Branton has provided food and drink for the villagers for the past four days.

From sunrise until dark, the whole village has pitched in—men, women and children. Right through the harvest the women and the children stayed out in the fields tying the wheat into sheaves to dry. When the field was full of sheaves of wheat, one of the children would run to the farm and tell old Billy Barnstaple to come. It was his job to bring the oxen-pulled cart into the field and load the sheaves until they were so high some inevitably toppled over. It became a game for the children as they ran along next to the cart, and their laughter filled the air. Amelia joined in and I was pleased to see her laughing.

It made me smile too and I was able to dispel my worry for a while.

I know Branton doesn't want me to go, and if I am honest, I could stay happily here for the rest of my life. He doesn't understand why I must leave. I must take Amelia home.

Despite the work of the harvest, and our weariness, each night we have been late going up to his rooms, and he has used all sorts of persuasions to convince me to stay. I won't write them here, as it would make any reader of my words blush. Those moments between us are private, and I will cherish them for as long as I live.

But the memories are in my head and lodged in my heart and my soul. And no matter where I am, I will never forget these months. The thought of leaving him is breaking my heart, but I have to go.

I love him and I am unsure if I will be able to go through with it.

Time is fleeting. Seize each opportunity. Make the most of every minute.

Alice jumped as there was a knock on the door. She pulled her robe across her gently swelling stomach. 'Come,' she called.

Mistress Oatley entered the room holding a candle.

'Mistress Alice, I am sorry to disturb you, but Mistress Irvine is downstairs in the parlour and says that it is urgent that she sees you immediately. I told her to come back in the morn, but the woman is distraught and said she must see you now.'

'Very well.' Alice nodded as she climbed down off the bed. 'Tell her I will be down shortly.'

It didn't take long to pull a cloak over her night attire, and Alice closed the door behind her as she hurried downstairs in her bare feet.

Mary was in the parlour, her face pale and set in a worried frown.

'Mary, what it is?'

The woman clenched her hands. 'Oh, Alice, I can't stop her. Amelia came to tell me that she plans to leave tonight.'

'What!' Alice clutched at Mary's arm. 'Where is she now? Has she gone to the stones already?'

'She is already there. I followed her there; I cannot talk sense into the foolish child. When I left to come here, she was touching the stone where she said she must.'

'Why? What does she think she is doing? It's the wrong time.'

'The poor girl does not want you to go with her. She said your life and your time is here now. She overheard that you are with child when you were talking to Lord Branton at the festival today. Will you come with me now and tell her it is not the right time? Who knows what danger she will find herself in?'

'Of course. I will get my shoes. It is warm enough to wear this light cloak. I will tell Mistress Oatley to let Lord Branton know that I had to go and see Amelia. Hopefully I shall return before he is home from the village.'

##

A short time later, Alice and Mary ran down the hill from the path towards the stones. The moon was full, and it was light enough for them to see Amelia sitting there with her face turned towards the middle stone.

Mary stumbled as they were halfway across the field. 'Oh, I've twisted my ankle. You go and get the silly girl, and I will catch you up.'

'Amelia. Step back,' Alice called out as she walked towards the stones.

'No. Alice, go home. I can do this by myself.'

'Don't be foolish. We will both go in three days at noon when it is the right time. You could end up anywhere.'

'I am going now,' Amelia said mutinously as Alice approached.

Alice's mouth dried as the familiar humming began and the stone began to glow and pulsate.

'Amelia, no! Move away,' she cried out as she grabbed for the young girl's hand.

As their fingers touched, Alice closed her eyes as the world spun around her. She held onto Amelia as tightly as she could. The humming increased and they were surrounded by a blue light. Her body stretched and her vision contracted. Alice closed her eyes and the darkness came.

Chapter 28
Branton

'Sard!' The curse broke from Branton's lips and he grabbed the banister of the stair rail leading to the upper storey of the manor. He'd kicked his toe on the bottom step of the staircase when it had appeared in front of him sooner than he expected. For a moment he considered sitting on the bottom step to nurse his now throbbing toe, but then decided if he sat down, his mead-addled head would probably not allow him to stand again.

He put his hand over his mouth. 'Must be quiet,' he mumbled. Branton knew he was well in his cups, and his challenge was to get to the top of the stairs, make his way down to the bedchamber and crawl into bed with Alice.

Robert had escorted him up the hill and had left him at the door of the manor. He had not drunk as much mead as Branton, but they had still sung bawdy songs together all the way from the village.

Happiness filled Branton. The harvest had produced the best yield for many years, he had the love of a wonderful woman, and she was carrying his child, and tonight—before he had drunk the last few tankards of mead—he had spoken to Robert of his dilemma, and Robert had come up with a solution.

He would tell Alice in the morn why she had no need to travel with Amelia. Grabbing the bannister, he pulled himself up the stairs. The hall was dark apart from a shaft of moonlight lighting the end near the door to the bedchamber. Lurching down the hall, Branton managed to open the door, cross to the large bed against the far wall, and collapse on top of the bed linen, still in the clothes he had worn all day.

Within seconds he was snoring, unaware of the empty space in the bed beside him.

##

With a dry mouth and a thumping head, Branton crawled out of bed at dawn the next morning. The bed was empty; Alice must have risen early. He frowned, hoping that his snoring hadn't disturbed her sleep. Crossing to the jug of water on the dresser, he sluiced his face and neck, and then stripped off his clothes. Reaching for a clean pair of breeches and a fresh tunic, he hurried to dress so he could talk to Alice.

The manor was quiet as he made his way down to the parlour where he knew Alice liked to sit and watch the sunrise. Branton was sheepish; his drunkenness last night was a rare event and he worried that it may have upset Alice. The parlour was empty, and he headed for the kitchen, where he could hear Mistress Hodges singing. He was pleased that Alice spent much of her time with the cook, and he was pleased that she had already garnered respect from his cook and housekeeper.

'Good morrow, Mistress Hodges.' He greeted her with a smile as he entered.

'My lord.'

'Have you seen Mistress Alice this morning?'

'No, I don't believe she has risen yet.'

'She may be in the garden. I shall look there.'

Branton stepped out onto the cobblestones as Robert walked out of the stable, his clothes askew and hay in his hair.

He too looked sheepish. 'I decided to sleep in the hay rather than risk the walk home.'

Branton chuckled. 'It was a very satisfactory harvest and festival.

'Have you spoken to Mistress Alice yet?'

Branton shook his head. 'No. I am looking for her now. She must have risen very early. I thought she might be out here in the herb garden.'

'I have not seen her,' Robert said as he headed towards the gate. 'I will see you in the fields later in the day.'

A niggle of concern worried at Branton as he walked through the house, and the front garden, and there was still no sign of Alice. For a wild moment, he thought she may have left without telling him and he ran back upstairs, but her precious notebook was open on the small table by the bed and he knew she would not leave that behind.

Branton glanced down, and dread pooled in his stomach as he read the words at the end of her latest entry.

And no matter where I am, I will never forget these months. The thought of leaving him is breaking my heart, but I have to go.

'Mistress Oatley!' His voice was loud as he ran down the long hall.

Where in Hades was the blasted woman?

'Mistress Oatley!' he called again.

As he reached the bottom of the stairs, his housekeeper appeared in the doorway, a bag over her arm.

'My lord? What is it?'

'Have you seen Mistress Alice?' he demanded.

'No. I went to the market at dawn. She had not risen when I left, and I assumed she would be tired from last night.'

'What happened last night?'

'Mistress Irvine came to see her to tell her she had to visit Amelia. She asked me to tell you where she had gone if you returned home before she did.'

'And did she?' He looked intently at the housekeeper and she put her head down.

'I am not sure, my lord. I am ashamed to say I fell asleep.'

Branton ran a hand through his hair, unsure of what to do.

'I will be back in an hour. If she returns, please send Hodges to the village to tell me.' He raced to the stables and jumped onto Black's back, not even talking time to put the saddle on

Putting his head down he grabbed the mane and spurred his stallion on towards the village.

Chapter 29

'Alice! Alice! Wake up, Please.'

Alice rolled over and opened her eyes. Nausea roiled in her stomach and a dull ache pulled at her lower back. The sky was beginning to lighten as the sun crept towards the eastern horizon.

She looked up at Amelia who was standing above her, worry filling her young face. 'Where are we?' she asked.

'We're at the stones,' Amelia said. 'Oh, Alice! Why did you have to grab me as I was leaving? I didn't want you to come with me.'

The memory of the night before slammed into Alice as she sat up and put her hand to her aching back. 'When are we?' she whispered.

'I don't know,' Amelia said but I did hear an aeroplane in the distance before, and I saw car lights and heard an engine just before you woke up.'

'Very well.' Alice stood and the pain in her back eased as she straightened, but her head was still spinning. 'Do you feel alright? Is your head dizzy?'

'No, I feel well.'

'Please help me up. We must be very careful. We will walk across the field and see if my cottage is there.'

'Can I just go to my place?'

'Amelia,' Alice said gently. 'We have to see where we are first. According to Mary we should have left at noon, the same time we left to go over. We could have come back at a time when things are different. You have to prepare yourself.'

The young girl's lip quivered in the growing light. 'I'm sorry, I just wanted to go home.'

'Whatever happens, at least we are together,' Alice kept her voice brisk, even though she was feeling quite ill. 'Now, come.'

As they stood together staring across the field, Alice's hope rose as she saw the two cottages sitting side by side. Both were in darkness but if she squinted her eyes, she would swear that she could see some smoke curling from Mr Jenkins' chimney.

'There is my cottage. We will go down the side of the cottage next door, but we must be quiet.'

For all they knew, the war could be over and there may have been an invasion. Alice swallowed as they set off towards the cottages and tried to ignore the constant ache in her back.

There *was* smoke curling from the Jenkins' cottage, but all was quiet as they crept down the side.

The grass at the front of Violet Cottage was long and the garden was full of weeds.

'Crouch down outside the wall, and I will see if I can find the key. Wait here until I call you,' she whispered to Amelia who did as she was told.

Alice pushed the gate open slowly and stopped it when it was only half open before it could creak. She slipped through the narrow space and walked towards the front porch.

All seemed quiet and still inside, but she jumped and put a hand to her chest as a blackbird trilled at the promise of dawn. Her heart was beating fast as she crouched and pulled at the cobblestone and she smiled as her hand encountered the cold metal key.

Taking a deep breath, Alice slid the key into the lock and turned it slowly. Goose bumps ran up her arms as she pushed the door half open not knowing what she would encounter.

What if it was before the war, and she and her parents still lived here? A wave of dizziness assailed her at that thought and she rested her head on the wooden door trying to raise the courage to go inside.

A sharp pain gripped her stomach, and dread consumed her.

Her child.

The travel had not been good for the baby. Taking another deep breath, she pushed the door fully open and peered around into the dim room.

The house smelled musty but sweet relief flooded through her as she saw the small case she had left on the sofa.

Was it yesterday? Or was it a long time ago? She had been gone for three seasons. And then she remembered the long grass at the gate.

Alice shook her head, she had to start thinking in 1941 words now. She had become used to the language of the Middle Ages.

Crossing the living room and stepping into the kitchen, she spotted the two food parcels on the table. The apples were shrivelled and all that remained of the cake were crumbs where a mouse or a rat had nibbled at it.

So, some time had passed.

She quickly walked up the stairs, holding her hand to her back and checked that the top floor was empty.

All was as she had left it.

Now all she had to do was get Amelia home, wait for noon and go back to Branton. There was nothing for her here, and she was keen to go back immediately.

Chapter 30
Branton – September 1497

Branton's world had changed. His interest in the estate died the morning after the harvest festival when he found that Alice had left him.

Without saying goodbye.

The grief that had consumed him had eventually turned to anger, but still he grieved the loss of the woman he had loved, and the child that he would never see.

On a cold and bleak spring night a year after Alice had left him, Branton sat in the dark stables with a flagon of mead as he brooded on the situation with the Pretender. Since two thousand Cornishmen had died at the Battle of Blackheath in June, he wondered at the futility of the political situation he had become involved in.

Damn you, Alice, he cursed for the thousandth time as he lifted the tankard. If she had stayed, all would have been well. He would have been happy; their child would have been born and he would not be involved in this futile battle.

It was time to go back to the estate and forget about the politics. And to forget about the woman he had loved, and who had left him.

It was time to marry Isabelle Davies and begin to make a life for himself again.

'My lord?'

Branton lifted his head and looked with a bleary eye at the man who stood in the door of the stables.

'What is it?' he asked impatiently.

'My lord, we have found a Cornishwoman hiding near the road. We believe she is spying for the Pretender.'

'Where is she now?' Branton pushed the tankard away and stood.

'She is here.' Two men walked in, each holding an arm of the woman between them. She lifted her head and looked at Branton and he stared.

He turned to the men and his voice was harsh. 'Be gone. Leave us alone.'

Branton's heart thudded and joy flooded through him in an almost unbearable wave. When the men were outside, he moved closer to the woman he thought he had lost forever.

'Alice? By the gods, Alice! You came back?'

He pulled her close and her face pressed into the rough wet wool of his cloak. He cradled his hand on the back of her headpiece unable to believe that she was here.

Words failed Branton for a long while as his body trembled, and Alice stood still and quiet in his arms.

'I have missed you so much.' His fingers gripped her waist, but he kept his hold gentle. 'I thought I had lost you. Oh, Alice—' His voice shook, and he rested his forehead against hers until she pressed her hands on his forearms and stepped back.

'Where am I?' she asked softly.

He looked at her closely. 'Your voice is different, and the lilt of your words has changed, Alice.'

Branton's world tilted as she looked up at him with sad eyes and her words broke his heart. 'No. I am not Alice. I am her niece. I have heard that I resemble her.'

He lowered his voice. 'Why do you lie, my sweet? What are you afraid of, Alice?'—the pleading in his voice was out of his control— 'you know I would never hurt you.'

'I am not Alice. I do not know you.'

She was watching him intently and he frowned. 'But Alice was alone; she had no family.' He lowered his brows. 'Or that was the truth I was told.'

'She was my grandfather's second cousin and we have always called her great aunt,' the woman said. 'When did Alice tell you that? When did she visit you?'

'You left me in autumn, but you— she—' he swallowed as disbelief and confusion replaced his joy— 'went after the harvest festival. You left my bed in the dark of night, Alice. You were not there when I woke the next morn. Why?'

'When was this, which wheat harvest? How long ago?'

His brow creased in a frown. 'Last autumn. A full year ago.'

'But when?' she insisted. 'What year was it?'

'Last September in the year of our Lord, 1496.'

He caught her as she fell in a dead faint.

***

In the soft light from the lamp burning on a small table in front of the window seat in the parlour, it was hard to see the woman's expression.

'Are you with me? Your thoughts seem a hundred miles away.' Alice's relative looked across at him. 'What shall I call you?'

'Branton is my name. Lord Branton of Brue Manor. And yours?'

'Beth,' she replied.

'Elisabeth?'

'No, just Beth. And I am well, thank you. I have received a couple of shocks today, and it is not like me to faint.'

'You are not Alice. I knew that when I carried you into the parlour.' The sadness and the loss of hope had left a physical ache in his chest. 'Do you know where Alice is? Is she well? Is she happy?'

Beth smoothed her fingers over her cloak. She took a breath and lifted her head and held his gaze. Her eyes were sad, and she hesitated before she spoke, but he knew what she was going to tell him

'Alice has passed on.'

Branton couldn't hold back the cry of grief that tore from his throat. When he looked up, tears were rolling down Beth's cheeks.

She moved along the window seat and took his hand. She was so much like Alice, his love, it was hard to look at her. 'I can tell you that she loved you, and that it broke her heart to leave you. I read her journals and she wrote how much she loved you and how hard it was to leave you.'

Her voice was soft. 'She said . . . "*no matter where I am, I will never forget these months. The thought of leaving him is breaking my heart, but I have to go*".'

'Is that why you came? To tell me she has gone?'

'In a way, perhaps it was,' Beth said slowly. 'I did not mean to come here.'

'Thank you.' He lifted his head and schooled his features into blankness even as his heart withered within him. 'Let us not speak of it again. I am sorry for the way my men treated you. But why were you on the road so late in the night? It is not a safe time for anyone to be travelling,'

Beth shook her head, put up a hand to cover a yawn 'It's a long story. I have travelled a long way today.'

'I am sorry. I have been most unwelcoming. I will call my housekeeper and she will take you to a guest room upstairs. Wait here.' He rose and went to the door and rang a bell.

'Thank you. I would appreciate that.' Beth went to stand as he did, but he gestured for her to remain where she was.

Mrs Oatley must have been hovering outside the door as she appeared straight away. She had taken excellent care of Branton in the past year, as had Mistress Hodges. He knew that they had both missed Alice too.

'Would you please bring us some refreshments, and prepare a room for our guest,' Branton asked.

They sat quietly and it wasn't long before Mistress Oatley brought a tray of food and placed it on the table beside the lamp. She looked at Beth and her face paled and she let out a small gasp as her hand went to her chest.

'It is not Mistress Alice,' he said sadly, but still she stared at the visitor as she backed out of the room.

Branton gestured to the tray; he was still finding it hard to look at her. 'I need to go and see to my horses.

When you are ready, ring the bell and Mistress Oatley will take you upstairs.' He needed time alone, before he spoke more to this woman.

He knew she was a traveller too.

'Would you tell me one thing before you leave me?' she asked.

He paused and nodded. 'If I can.'

'Tell me why it is not safe? What is happening. Is it a war? Is there a battle?'

It was almost as though she already knew something and was not telling him.

'There is no war yet, but there may be. A Pretender's Cornish army is advancing on Taunton, only twenty miles from here.' He sat rigid and clenched his hands in front of him. 'Two thousand Cornishmen died at the Battle of Blackheath in June. I do not want to see innocent men die again.'

'You were there?'

'I was.' He nodded. 'When Alice left me, I lost interest in my estate. I handed it over to my man, Robert, to look after and joined the defenders.'

'But you are back now?

'Yes. Seeing the futility of that battle made me realise that my place is here, looking after my tenants, and my crops and my sheep. I don't want to see that happen again, so it is imperative that you stay here until the danger is over.'

'But—'

He held up his hand. 'We will speak more tomorrow. Please be assured you are safe while ever you are in my house.' Beth stood and he grasped her hands. 'You have given me sad news today, but I have closure and I thank you for that.'

Chapter 31
Alice - October 1948

Alice sighed as she opened her notebook for what could be the last time. She had filled three notebooks since she had come back to the cottage seven years ago, and it was time to store them in a trunk in case anyone was interested in what had become of her if her research had been successful.

It must be, Alice thought, clenching her hands before she picked up her pencil. *I have to get back to Branton.*

Her understanding of the physics of what she had read was not deep, but Alice had enough understanding of Einstein's theory to be confident; hours and hours at the British Library had informed her.

How light appeared when an observer is accelerating, and that the occurrence of solar and lunar eclipses created a dip in the space and time continuum. Being located on one of the magnetic ley lines at the time created an opening. Alice nodded. She had enough faith in what she had learned to try one last time.

Much soul searching, and seven years of planning and putting my affairs in order, and now I am here again. I have no doubt that Branton will be waiting for me.

The seven years that had passed since she had taken Amelia home safely to her family had not been kind to Alice. The pains during the night she had travelled had been a warning of the miscarriage that had occurred the following day.

Despite their joy at having Amelia brought home to them, the Adnums had been very kind, and had taken care of her after Alice had come home from the cottage hospital in Glastonbury. She had been inconsolable at the loss of her child, as she had been when she discovered that Mr Jenkins had passed in the winter she had been away, and her grief had intensified. A new couple lived in the cottage next door, but Alice kept her distance.

War still raged in Europe and the bombings were as frequent as they had been when she had left. She missed Branton as much as that part of her had been lost with the baby. The war endured for another four years.

The worst part was dealing with the grief of Mother and Daddy being gone all over again, and I had withdrawn into myself and become frail, in both body and mind, she wrote in her final entry.

The worst part was the number of times I went to the stones and touched them, but they remained cold and dead beneath my hands.

Seven endless years of heart-numbing grief and wondering if I should have stayed with him.

The grief of leaving Branton behind had been unbearable, and when I came home to the cottage, and found I was unable to travel back, I immersed myself in volunteer work. I joined the Land Army; during the war there was always plenty to do and I trained at Cannington Farm as a land girl. It was easier for me than many of the young women who came down from London, but it was safer than being in the city with the daily bombings.

It was bad enough in the country, and even Somerset was bombed. The farm I was allocated to was three miles out of Yeovil beneath the flight path of the German bombers coming from the west of France.

Air raid sirens became a part of our lives, but strangely, my grief made me immune to the reactions of those around me. At that time in my life, death held no fear for me. It wasn't until the war was over that I managed to pull myself out of the numb state where I spent much of those years. Wearying years where a sense of desperate urgency held the population in its relentless grip, then stolid endurance through the Blitz, and the ever-growing fear of invasion. But then the tide turned as hope came from a North African victory, and we began to believe that the end may be near.

In a way, volunteering eased my guilt at having gone away when the war began. I wasn't a coward; none of us expected the war to last for so long. No one had imagined the bombing, and the damage to our countryside. The displaced children, and the lack of men to work the farms.

Toiling alongside other young women in the field helped me to forget and some days I managed to go for hours without thinking of what I had left behind.

Perhaps I should not have followed Mistress Irvine that night. But I look now at Amelia, and her parents, and know that even though my loss was immense, I did the right thing

But if I had stayed, perhaps our child may have survived.

I will never know.

During the seven years that Alice had tried to cross back to Branton and failed, Amelia had been a pillar of strength to Alice. The poor child carried heavy guilt for Alice's situation, and she spent much time with her. Now Amelia was grown and had married a local farmer, Alice knew it was time for her to succeed in her quest to return to Branton. She had done it before; she would do it again. Amelia's family had accepted her explanation of what had happened, yet had mourned the loss of those years they had lost with her.

In the end it had been simple. After months of research in the British Library, Alice had worked out the cause and effect of the solar and lunar eclipses on the ley lines.

Today, the 17th October 1948, the penumbral lunar eclipse would occur and would be followed by a solar eclipse in two weeks. The same pattern of time and eclipses that had occurred during the harvest when she had left Branton in 1496.

The night before Alice would attempt to travel back to Branton she woke in the middle of the night, her cheeks wet with tears. She had dreamed of going back and her heart had broken in her dream.

She got out of bed and made her way down to the kitchen and filled the kettle with water, trying to calm the beating of her heart.

In her dream Branton had been dead. The dream had been so real, and she pulled out her dairy to record it while it was fresh in her mind.

I longed to see the roses and the honeysuckle that climbed his manor house, almost as much as I longed to see Branton. I thought that I would have many years to see that.

This time I would stay and make my life with him. It had taken many, many hours of soul searching to come to that decision, but the love I held for him in my heart was too strong to ignore. I knew it was a lifetime but—

Suddenly a huge whoosh and a deafening noise filled the air around me.

I ran. I pushed through the hedgerow into the field beside the road in case there was another explosion.

I backed away as the hoarse cries of men in pain surrounded me. Dozens of men lay on the ground in front of me. I tried to lift my feet but the mud that had been churned by many feet held my leather shoes like a steel vice.

I raised a shaking hand to my lips and stifled a cry. One moment I had been walking alone and thinking of the delightful reunion ahead, and then I had been thrown off my feet by an explosion and a force so strong my chest still ached.

The scene before me was carnage such as I had never witnessed before. It was like the photos that I had seen of the battlefields in the First World War, in the trenches of France where my maternal grandfather had perished.

As I stood there, a young man, no older than my sister's son—Alice frowned as she wrote of her dream; she had no sister—*rolled over onto his back and held his hands out to me, beseeching me to help him. His face was a rictus of pain and blood dripped into his eyes.*

I closed my eyes knowing it was all a dream.

It is only a dream, Alice told herself, even as her chest still ached with the loss of Branton.

Maybe I hadn't come here after all, but the heartrending cries could not have come from my imagination or dreams. I sank to the ground, not caring about the cold mud on my skirts, and I held out my hands to comfort the dying young man.

It was a full week before I made my way to Glastonbury and the manor house, but it was empty. The door was locked and there was no smoke from the chimneys, the house was in disrepair and it looked as though it hadn't been lived in for many weeks.

I knocked but there was no one there. The stables were empty, and there was no life anywhere.

No chickens pecking the grass around the stables, and the fields were empty of sheep.

Branton was gone.

I choked back my despair as I retraced my steps towards home.

##

It was a *dream,* Alice told herself over and over.

Putting down the now cold tea, she came to a decision.

If she didn't go back, she would never know, and this was the correct time to travel according to her research.

This time I will stay and make my life with him. It has taken many, many months to come to that decision, but the love I hold for him in my heart is too strong to ignore.

He will be there.

She closed the notebook and put it into the trunk. It was time.

Alice packed. She had carefully put aside the clothes she had worn seven years ago. They had been washed and folded and kept in mothballs. She changed and smiled as she looked down at the clothes that Mistress Oatley had brought from the market in Glastonbury for her.

Closing the door of the cottage behind her, and slipping the key beneath the cobblestone, Alice made her way across the field to the three stones, anticipation and joy dismissing any lingering doubt.

The light was dying, and Branton would be in from the fields.

Dear God, she prayed as her dream once again filled her thoughts. Please let him be there.

Chapter 32
Branton – October 17, 1503

Branton came in from the stables and nodded at Mistress Budden. The death of his long serving cook, Mistress Hodges a year ago, followed by the death of King Henry's wife, Elizabeth of York and their baby daughter, Princess Katherine, had created a black mood in him that had lasted many months.

Since the brief visit of Alice's kinswoman, he had accepted that Alice was lost to him forever. Perhaps that is why she had crossed the time gate that Alice had spoken of, so he could accept that Alice, his love, would never return.

But no matter how much Isabelle Davies had pressed over the past seven years, Branton had not been inclined to marry.

The last blackness that he had suffered this year had taught him that he must get on with his life. Tomorrow, he would ask his friend, Robert, for Isabelle's hand in marriage.

Branton dined on a fine meal—Mistress Budden was a fine cook— and then he took his tankard out to the new terrace that Hodges had built while he was trying to cope with the loss of his wife. He sat on the low stone wall, still warm from the autumn sun and surveyed his estate.

Harvest was over and the autumn was coming. The poem that Alice had recited to him seven autumns ago had always stayed in his mind.

'While barred clouds bloom the soft-dying day,
And touch the stubble-plains with rosy hue;
Then in a wailful choir the small gnats mourn.'

The gnats were mourning tonight in a loud chorus, and it pleased Branton to see the stubbled fields touched rose by the late setting sun. It had been another good harvest and now the countryside around him held the vibrant golds and reds that autumn had bestowed.

It was at this time of the year that he felt closest to Alice. Branton looked heavenward and sent a prayer up that wherever she was, in life or death, that she was happy. As he lowered his gaze, a bright flash came from the fields below, where the marker stones were, and he smiled, taking it as a sign that Alice was in a good place.

He sipped at his mead and stared at the stones as a small figure stepped from behind the middle stone. As the figure came closer, Branton stood and his tankard dropping unheeded to the cobblestones.

Indescribable joy filled his soul as Alice walked up the hill towards him. His limbs trembled as disbelief held him in its thrall and he rubbed his eyes, but when Branton removed his hands, she was closer, and he could see the smile on his love's face.

It was not Beth.

It was his Alice.

Happiness lent wings to Branton's feet, and he ran down the hill to meet her.

He stood before her and they looked at each other without words for a long time.

Branton cupped Alice's face in his hands as she looked up at him. Her soft, sweet lips parted, and he lowered his mouth to hers.

As he took her lips in a gentle kiss, time fell away. It no longer mattered that they had been apart. The kiss healed their loss in a way that words would never replace. His hands rested on either side of her beautiful face as he pulled back and drank in his fill of the love that shone from her eyes. His thumb caressed her cheek as their breaths mingled. Branton pulled her nearer until they were as close as they could be, and he could feel the beating of his heart against her chest.

Slow and steady, in time with his, promising the future.

'I came home, my dear heart,' Alice said. 'It took me a long time to find my way, but I came home.'

Epilogue

Alice and Branton lived together happily as man and wife for over twenty years, until Branton passed in 1523 during the English invasion of France. Sadly, he was not there to fight, but was in Paris selling wool from Brue Manor.

Eventually, Alice decided there was no reason to stay without Branton—she knew her grief would be more bearable if she was away from Brue Manor, and close memories of her life with Branton.

Alice travelled home, and learned more of the ley lines, and her ability to traverse time, when she arrived back at Violet Cottage in 1968 and met Davy Morgan.

***

If you would like to read more of their story, and the travels of the McLaren family, the final book in the

Love Across Time series, *The Threads that Bind* will be published in 2021.

You can pre-order it here:

https://www.annieseaton.net/store.html

Sign up to Annie's newsletter on her website to stay up to date with publication dates.

https://www.annieseaton.net/

A teaser for you from Book 1, *Come Back to Me*, available now

COME BACK TO ME

Megan found the key where Beth had said it would be. She turned it with trembling fingers, and it unlocked the door with surprising ease. Exhaustion claimed her and as soon as she switched the light on, she headed for the first chair. Old fashioned floral fabrics and an overpowering smell of camphor filled the room and she slumped gratefully into the soft sofa.

She leaned her head back and groaned. The train had been late and when the taxi had finally dropped her at the cottage, she'd been unable to find the key where it was supposed to be. She'd pulled out her phone, but it was dead, and she couldn't charge it till she got inside, so she'd decided to camp out on the porch of the cottage until daylight and then head into the village to call Tony. From the distance, the muted sound of music reached her through the still air and her skin tingled with anticipation as she realised she was hearing the rehearsal from the festival.

And, of course, she'd ended up at the wrong bloody cottage. Why had things suddenly begun going so wrong for her? Ever since her parents' accident, nothing in her life had seemed to go right.

She closed her eyes to rest…for a brief moment, and then she'd go back and get her suitcase. God, she was so tired. She'd gotten a lot of work done on the twenty-two-hour flight across from Australia but going more than twenty-four hours without sleep, and worrying about her appeal, had drained her. It had taken five hours to get out of terminal two at Heathrow and make her way across London to Paddington Station. She'd almost—only almost—been too tired to even appreciate being in *London.* A place she'd dreamed of visiting her whole life.

Then, at the almost-deserted railway station it seemed as though she'd waited for hours for an old black cab to drive her down the never-ending country lanes until they had finally reached the cottage.

The wrong damn cottage.

Her face heated as she remembered the reception she'd gotten from the dark and brooding David Morgan.

When the light had first shone on his face and she'd seen those deep blue eyes staring at her, her heart had almost stopped beating. Davy Morgan had been her idol when she'd been in her early teens and she knew his face intimately. She'd scoured the retro shops and had found posters of him as well as David Bowie, Queen, Bryan Ferry, and Duran Duran to cover her bedroom walls. While all her friends had been into nineties bands, she had loved listening to all the compilation CDs of seventies music, and she'd uploaded them all to her iPod. She was sure she'd been born in the wrong time.

She grinned to herself. The posters of his uncle were still rolled up somewhere in a box along with her CDs of all his albums. She even had her parents' old vinyl records stowed away. In a special place—in her flat, and in her heart— was the record that Dad had bought for her on the day her parents had been killed.

Davy Morgan's songs had started her love affair with music. She hadn't even heard of this nephew, David Morgan, but if he was playing at Glastonbury, he must have some claim to fame. Probably cashing in on the fame of his uncle.

But he'd assumed she was a groupie, so he must have some fame of his own.

But what a jerk. Heat filled her cheeks as she recalled his words. A shag, for goodness sake,

Wham, bam, thank you, ma'am. He wasn't even original. She knew her Bowie song lyrics, thank you very much.

And God, he was her neighbour. She hoped like hell he wasn't around when she went back to collect her bag. She'd just rest her eyes for a minute before she went back to get her bag, and *then* find a bed.

Alone in Violet Cottage.

The sun filtering through the narrow paned window and the twittering of an unfamiliar bird woke Megan. She lay on the soft sofa, pondering the birdsong, before the events of the previous day came crashing back. Closing her eyes, she groaned at the memory of last night and how she had ended up at the wrong house.

Megan cleared her mind, focusing on her breathing until her consciousness was directed inward. After a few moments, she was aware only of her inhaling and exhaling, until the tightness in her chest began to ease. Keeping her eyes closed, she let snatches of songs float through her mind. It was a technique she had perfected through her grief last year and she could now achieve it without any external aids.

No candles, no music. Just her own thoughts. Good thoughts.

She dozed again and woke a short time later, refreshed and calm. The sun was still shining in the window and the same bird was trilling away happily. Wandering through the small cottage, she smiled at the contrast to her own apartment, which was always cluttered with books, papers, and music.

This little place was filled with knickknacks and crocheted doilies and dozens of framed photos. She climbed the narrow stairs and peeked into the two small bedrooms. The one facing the east was full of sunshine and she chose that one for her stay. Sitting on the bed, a wide grin broke across her face as she sank into the soft bedding, which was covered with a white candlewick bedspread.

She was in a cottage in the English countryside. It was all she could do not to break into a happy dance. Huge pink roses and trailing tendrils of green leaves papered the wall. She crossed the room to the window and looked across at the other cottage.

Rose Cottage was only a short distance away, across the emerald-green grass and a low fence. Too close for her peace of mind, but she'd just ignore the guy next door. Pushing the window open, she leaned out. The two small cottages were surrounded by open green fields with a narrow road lined with hedgerows winding away into the distance. On the horizon, the hill she knew from her research was Glastonbury Tor rose above the distant village. Church roofs and spires glinted in the bright sunlight and a sense of well-being stole over her as her problems receded. It was like coming home. In the field at the back of the cottages were three tall stone markers and Megan grinned. She wouldn't even have to take a tour to nearby Stonehenge now. It looked as though there were Neolithic monuments almost in the back garden.

Bright yellow roses tumbled over the fence between the two homes and in the distance, she could see the tents and stage being set up for the festival on the farm at Pilton. A frisson of anticipation ran through her and she smiled. She planned on heading over to have a look at the festival site as soon as she got settled, but first she had to go next door and collect her suitcase. Hopefully, *he'd* gone out.

Going back down the steep wooden staircase to the ground floor of the cottage, she wandered into the kitchen. A huge ancient Aga stove filled the whole wall next to the door. She picked up the kettle and turned the tap at the old stone sink.

Nothing. Apart from a few creaks and groans and spits of rusty water. Opening the old refrigerator, she was pleased to see a jug of water and filled the kettle from that. It took a bit of fiddling to get the stove going but after a while she had a little gas flame alight. It would take a few minutes before the cold water in the kettle heated enough to have a coffee so she went into the small bathroom next to the kitchen to give her face a quick wash. But the tap there produced no water either. After running her fingers through her mussed hair, she straightened her now-crumpled T-shirt and jeans and went back into the kitchen. The whistling kettle was bubbling merrily on the stove and she switched the flame off and scrabbled through the cupboards for coffee.

Nothing. Not even a tea bag. Beth had said the cottage was rented out for the odd weekend, and she thought there might have been some coffee or tea bags, at least, in the cupboard. It looked like a walk into the village for some essentials was her first task for the day.

No, the second. First job was to collect her suitcase from next door and then, even if she couldn't wash, she could at least put on some clean clothes.

The sunshine was bright and warm at her back, although nowhere near as warm as summer in Sydney. Megan appreciated the fresh air and the sweet smell of the grass and the bluebells lining the path. Her heart beat a little faster as she walked slowly through the gate and along the footpath to the cottage next door, but there was no sign of life. The door was closed, and all the windows were shut.

Great. He'd gone out or he was still in bed.

She quickly retrieved the suitcase and turned to go back to her cottage.

The door behind her creaked open and she put her head down and kept going, determined to ignore him.

"Morning, sweets." She stopped walking and turned around. The posh accent was at odds with the sight of the laid-back man leaning against the doorframe who lifted his cup and nodded at her.

Megan's breath caught in her throat and she stared at him unabashedly. Tight, low-slung black jeans were unbuttoned, and his chest was bare. Her mouth dried as her gaze rose from his bare feet, up his legs, and skittered past the dark V of hair running into the top of his open jeans, and farther up to sleep-rumpled hair, with sexy dark stubble covering his strong jaw. He was a dead ringer for his uncle. He could have stepped straight from one of the posters that used to cover her walls.

"Cat got your tongue?"

Last night she hadn't noticed what a beautiful speaking voice he had. Deep and smooth with a melodious hint of a Welsh accent, but the hard line of his jaw and his closed expression didn't quite fit with the sexy voice. She held his gaze and drew a quick breath. Dark-blue eyes surrounded by long dark eyelashes stared back at her. His unsmiling gaze was fixed on her face, but she still self-consciously tugged her crumpled T-shirt down over her bare midriff without speaking.

"Ah, she has lost her voice." He said to no one in particular before tipping the mug to his mouth and taking a sip. The smell of freshly brewed coffee drifted across and Megan's nose twitched. She put her suitcase down and pulled herself up straight, meeting his gaze.

"No, I haven't lost my voice," she said. "I was wondering if I could speak to you without getting another crude proposition."

He laughed. "Up to you, sweetheart. But it wouldn't be a bad way to start the day, if you are interested. Guaranteed to get the blood pumping."

His gaze pinned her and as his lips tipped up, she realised he was teasing.

She knew she needed to lighten up. Her life for the past few months had made her way too serious.

"I came for my suitcase, but I wouldn't say no to one of those." She looked at the coffee cup in his hand. "I haven't had time to shop, and I thought there might be something in the cottage, but there's not even a stray tea bag."

"Not surprised. No one's been there all summer," he said. His intent gaze stayed on her face and Megan's neck prickled. There was something about this man that unsettled her. She'd come across arrogant musicians like him as she'd interviewed them for her research, but his resemblance to his uncle unnerved her.

"I suppose I can stretch to some coffee." He stepped through the door and she moved, about to follow him into his home, but he stopped her with a curt command over his shoulder. "Wait there."

Megan did as she was told, stayed on the porch and looked out over the green fields. If he didn't want her inside, that was fine by her. The less she had to do with the rude musician, the better for her peace of mind.

And God knows she needed peace, and nothing more to stress her.

The air was still and the sound of the bees buzzing in the roses in the cottage garden drifted across to her. A couple of minutes later, David appeared at the door with a different mug in his hand and passed it to her.

"Cream and sugar. You could do with fattening up."

Maybe, just maybe, there was a kind person beneath that aggressive exterior. He'd brought her coffee and in Megan's books that was one way to get in her good graces. Undeniably, there were good looks and a kind of charm…or rather a dangerous attraction. He stepped back inside and turned to her. "Keep the cup. Consider it a welcome gift."

The door shut in her face and all was quiet, apart from the bees and the occasional mooing of a cow.

Okay, take back the thoughts of him being kind or having basic manners.

No. No charm at all. The less I see of him, the better. Bemused, she shook her head and took a sip of the hot coffee before grabbing the handle of the suitcase and dragging it along the path back to her cottage.

Books 1 and 2 now available in print and eBook

Other Books
Signed copies are also available from Annie's online store in print

https://www.annieseaton.net/store.html

Whitsunday Dawn

Undara

Osprey Reef (2021)

Porter Sisters Series

Kakadu Sunset

Daintree

Diamond Sky

Hidden Valley (2021)

Pentecost Island Series

Pippa

Eliza

Nell

Tamsin

Evie

Cherry

Odessa

Sienna (2021)

Tess (2021)

Isla (2021)

Bondi Beach Love Series

Beach House

Beach Music

Beach Walk

Beach Dreams

The House on the Hill

Second Chance Bay Series

Her Outback Playboy

Her Outback Protector

Her Outback Haven

Her Outback Paradise

Love Across Time Series

Come Back to Me

Follow Me

Finding Home

The Threads that Bind (2021)

Others

The Trouble with Paradise

Deadly Secrets

Adventures in Time

Silver Valley Witch

The Emerald Necklace

Worth the Wait

Ten Days in Paradise

Acknowledgements

*A special thank you to my wonderful editor and
critique partner, Susanne Bellamy,
and my eagle-eyed proof-readers, Roby Aiken,
Anna Welch and Marcia Batton.*

About the Author

AWARDS

2014 - Author of the Year Ausrom Readers' Choice
2015 - Best Established Author Ausrom Readers' Choice
2016 - Finalist for Author of the Year, Book of the Year, Cover of the Year, Ausrom Readers' Choice
2016 – Finalist RWA Ruby Award: Kakadu Sunset-
2017 - Best Established Author, Ausrom Readers' Choice
2018 - Finalist NZ KORU Award: Her Outback Cowboy
2018 Book of the Year (Whitsunday Dawn) Ausrom Readers' Choice Awards
2019 - Finalist NZ KORU Award: Her Outback Haven

Annie lives in Australia, on the beautiful north coast of New South Wales. She sits in her writing chair and looks out over the tranquil Pacific Ocean. She has fulfilled her lifelong dream of becoming an author and is producing books at a prolific rate.

She writes contemporary romance and loves telling the stories that always have a happily ever after. She lives with her very own hero of many years and they share their home with Toby, the naughtiest dog in the universe, and Barney, the rag doll kitten, who hides when the grandchildren come to visit.

Stay up to date with her latest releases at her website: **http://www.annieseaton.net**

If you would like to stay up to date with Annie's releases, subscribe to her newsletter on her website.

www.ingramcontent.com/pod-product-compliance
Ingram Content Group UK Ltd.
Pitfield, Milton Keynes, MK11 3LW, UK
UKHW011651270625
6625UKWH00034B/124